Armand Rosamilia

IT'S 5 O'CLOCK SOMEWHERE

The GOLDEN LION CAFÉ

FLAGLER BEACH
FICTION SERIES

GOLDEN LION CAFÉ

Flagler Beach Fiction Series

Armand Rosamilia

Edited by Jenny Adams

Cover and Interior Photos by David Royall

Rymfire Books

http://armandrosamilia.com

Print Edition August 2013

Special Thanks to Tony, Tiki and the great staff of
Golden Lion Café for the help, the great food and the
Pusser's Painkillers…

David Royall for the great pictures of Golden Lion
Café and Jenny Adams for the great editing job… I
owe both of you (as usual)

And the many varied characters that make up the
unique sunny paradise that is Flagler Beach

Flagler Beach Fiction Series

Kokomo's Café

Golden Lion Cafe

J And J Fitness

Flagler Fish Company

Nerdz Comics And More

Sully's Surf Shop

Bahama Mama's

Golden Lion Café

Flagler Beach Fiction Series

It's My Job

Leslie, office manager for the Golden Lion Café, shook her head at the sight before her: Tommy, the owner, face on his desk, his laptop opened and off, a bottle of unopened rum and an empty glass before him.

"You're doing this all wrong," she said, as she shook him awake.

"Huh? What?" Tommy had a thick British accent and she always laughed when he slurred his words just after waking. More and more frequently, she'd been finding him here, slumped over his computer, when she came in to open the restaurant.

"I'm supposed to find you, asleep and drooling on your desk, with an empty bottle of rum or three. You need to smell like alcohol, not the cheese fries you ate at midnight. Can't you do anything right?"

Tommy laughed. "I s'pose I should have at least cracked the seal on the rum, right? Fill a bit in me glass, douse my gums with it to make the scene more charming." He flicked the laptop on. "That might be fun to add into me story, love."

"I'll leave you alone. Can I get you some coffee?"

Tommy looked at her and grinned. "After a long night of drinking? I'd love a cup."

Leslie closed his office door. He'd be in there for the next two hours, until eleven, when they would officially open, tapping away at his Great American Novel. *I s'pose it's his Great British Novel, love,* she thought with a laugh. Tommy was great to work for because he didn't micro-manage the staff. He let his managers do their job and, as long as he didn't have to step in with a problem, he didn't create any by being around. He spent most of his day in his office trying to write his novel, anyway.

This early - it was only nine - the only company Leslie had was the gulls, lined up on the upper deck, already trying to find the perfect spot for dropped food as the day wore on, and Chrissie, one of the waitresses. She always showed up two hours early when she was working the opening shift because she shared a car with her mom, who went to training at J and J Fitness at this time.

Chrissie smiled at Leslie and went back to reading her book, as she lounged at a picnic table.

"What are you reading?" Leslie asked. "I'm sure it's something with blood and guts in it."

Chrissie smiled and held up the book, a yellow cover with a nice beach scene.

"That doesn't look bad," Leslie said.

"You didn't look too closely, did you?"

Leslie wrinkled her face when she saw the woman on the cover was a zombie and had blood on her torso. She read the title. "*Dying Days?* Where do you find this crap?"

"This author is local. I'm going to find out where he lives and stalk him, see if I can be in his next book. His stories are set right here in Flagler Beach and up to Saint Augustine. You know where the stilt houses are near Matanzas Inlet? Most of the action is there. It's really good so far."

"No thanks. I'll stick to romance and non-fiction. You want a cup of coffee?"

"Tommy asleep in his office again?"

"Of course. It's Saturday. Where else would he spend a Friday night?"

"I'll take a cup. Today should be busy." Chrissie looked up at the clear sky. "The tourists are in town, and they'll love Flagler Beach. I hope I tip out nice; I need to buy groceries."

"I always hope the locals come in, too. A nice mix of people is always fun." Even though Leslie was the office manager, she spent most of the day, when they were open for business, on the floor. She tried to get all her orders and problem solving done before eleven so she had time to see how the flow was for the day and what needed to be ordered ahead of time. She hated to react to problems. Solving them before they happened was her strong suit. And making coffee, right now.

One of the bad things about her job, however, was call-outs. When she'd gotten the coffee brewing and the phone rang, she knew it was one of the first-shift waitresses or cooks. When she answered, she knew who it was immediately, because of the kids screaming in the background.

"Les, I gotta call out today. I got both little ones running a fever and they've been up all night. I'm really sorry to do this to you," Carole said. "I tried calling Chrissie to cover for me but she didn't answer."

"She's already working today. I'll call someone else in; don't worry about it." Leslie hung up. What could you do? As busy as they'd be today, being short-staffed wasn't an option. But there were enough waiters and waitresses who knew the cash pull of a clear day like this in the summer. She could probably call in three people without a problem.

For right now, she intended to get some paperwork done in her office and then start in on the coffee. She walked and dialed Amanda's number. She was technically a hostess but she was looking for more hours and had waitressing experience.

Amanda answered on the first ring and was excited to hear from Leslie. "I'll call you right back. I just need a sitter for my son."

Just as Leslie hung up, the phone rang again. It was one of the bus boys calling out, which she was not happy about. She'd have to have a sit down with him the next time he actually worked, because he was calling out more and more. That was the problem with hiring young kids: they did this for beer money, or because their parents wanted them to have a summer job. But, as soon as they got a paycheck or two under their belt, they thought they were rich and didn't need more money.

The only bus boy not working was Austin, who they called Man-Child because he was so big for his age. At seventeen, he had a full goatee and was a couple inches over six foot. He was a good kid and a fast learner. He'd also been promised today off, even though they were short-staffed in this area. Until they hired a couple more, it was everyone having to work five days a week.

When the phone had rung three times, Leslie was about to hang up and get some paperwork done now that she was at her desk.

"Hello?" a groggy Man-Child asked.

"Austin, don't kill me... but Jim called out today."

"You should fire him," Austin said simply.

Leslie smiled. She loved this kid, because he had no filter and said whatever was on his mind. He was big enough to get away with it, too. "Well, that's for another day. Right now, I need a bus boy for the mid-shift. I would really appreciate it."

Austin groaned on the phone.

"I would *really* appreciate it. I wouldn't ask you if I didn't think I really needed you."

"What's in it for me?" he asked.

Leslie smiled, knowing exactly what he was getting at. "Chrissie is working today. I'll give you her section."

"What? I don't care about that," he said, too quickly.

"So then I'll give her area to someone else?"

"If you want me to come in, you won't," Austin said and laughed. "Give me an hour. I need to make sure my mom can drop me off."

"If I don't hear from you, I'll assume you're coming in."

She could hear Austin screaming to his mom about getting a ride to work. "OK, I'll see you soon. Thanks."

Leslie looked at Chrissie, sitting at a table and reading, and she smiled. If the girl knew how many boys and men working at the Golden Lion Café and customers were into her, she'd die. She was so naïve and sweet; it would be a shame for a guy to take advantage of her.

The phone rang again. *Not on a Saturday*, she thought and frowned. Who was calling out now?

*　*　*　*　*

Leslie checked her watch. It wasn't even 9:30, yet. She now had three call-outs and the phone was ringing again. She usually posted the roster by this time, but she'd be wasting her time and crossing off names like mad.

"What is going on today? Is it too nice out, and no one wants to work?" She answered the phone. "Golden Lion, I hope you're not calling out," she said.

There was a pause on the line. "Shit, Les, don't say stuff like that. You're going to make me feel bad."

Leslie recognized Rodney's voice. "Guilty enough not to call out?"

"I can't. Sorry. I know it's last minute but our aunt passed away late last night. Heather and I need to go to Tampa and be with the family. Please don't kill us."

Leslie groaned. "Wow, I just lost both of you in one call."

"I'll put her on the line so she can officially tell you, so she doesn't get into trouble. Again, really sorry."

"I understand. You don't have to bother her. My prayers go with you and your family." Leslie hung up and pulled her own cell phone out, where she kept everyone's numbers for easy reference. She was running out of people to call in. Short staffing on a beautiful Saturday was not an option.

She called the new waiter, Andy, who'd only worked three shifts so far. He had experience, though. She knew he had worked for over two years at Flagler Fish Company before going to college, and he'd dropped out and come back but wanted to work somewhere different. "Andy? Leslie from The Golden Lion Café. Hey. What's the chance you can come in today? I have a couple of call-outs." Leslie smiled. "Perfect. Sure, I can pencil you in for eleven. Will it give you enough time?"

Leslie hung up and dwelled on what he'd said: he just needed to throw some clothes on and he'd be in. Despite her being almost twenty years his senior, she wasn't dead. The guy was hot. He could be a model, with a buff body and gorgeous blue eyes. He had a chiseled face and when he smiled he had Rob Lowe dimples. Even covered up in a yellow Golden Lion shirt, he was sex appeal on two muscular legs. He was quick to smile and was never overtly flirty but, you could tell he enjoyed the attention in a subtle way. Woody was nice enough to him, although, he called him Blockhead or Andy GQ when he wasn't around. Professional jealousy.

And the women fawned over him. Tommy noticed it during his first shift. "The lad's got some looks to him, right? I never looked like 'im at that age, din't I tell you? But, he better take advantage of it, since it won't last forever. Cheers to him."

Leslie realized she was daydreaming about a guy who could be her son. She still needed to find a replacement for Heather, too. And she was running out of options.

She made three calls to staff not on the schedule today, not surprised when no one picked up. She switched tactics and used her cell phone to call Amy, who rarely answered her phone.

When Amy answered, Leslie crossed her fingers. "Amy? It's Leslie. I really, really need you to cover a late shift today. Please," she added quickly. "I wouldn't ask if I didn't need you."

Amy laughed. "What time?"

"Last shift."

"I'll be over this hangover by then."

"What?"

"Busting your chops. Relax, Les."

"Oh, good. I thought you were serious."

"I did just get home from Orlando. I saw a killer show at the Hard Rock. I'll get in a nap and then a shower and try not to smell like beer. See ya later."

"I appreciate it." Everyone called her Crazy Amy but she wore the nickname with pride. She was a southern gal, born in Anderson, South Carolina, but she'd been in Florida for years. She was absolutely stunning with dark hair and a plethora of tattoos covering her arms, legs and other places many customers and staff had tried to see over the months. Amy was friendly but very reserved, unless you got her talking about seeing a kick ass band or tats. The last time she worked she was nursing a new tattoo she'd gotten on her elbow, and was afraid she'd bump the tender flesh.

Dave Sullivan, owner of Sully's Surf Shop, often came in during her shifts and compared new ink. Leslie couldn't remember who currently had more but, if Sully was winning, Amy would pay for his first drink, and, if Amy was ahead, he'd give her a double-tip. It worked for them, and everyone knew, eventually, the two would be hooking up.

Leslie went to her office, peeked in at the sleeping Tommy. She decided against slamming her palms on his desk and scaring the heck out of him, but it was very tempting. He'd sleep for another hour or so, until they started getting customers and the place got loud.

"Damn," she said under her breath. In all the excitement of phone calls, she never got coffee, and she was supposed to deliver a cup to him. She walked back to the bar area and Chrissie met her with two steaming Styrofoam cups of coffee. "Thanks. You read my mind."

"Actually, I could hear Tommy snoring even with his door closed. I know the only thing that wakes him up is a cup of coffee.

And, I know when you get busy on the phone, you always forget. You're welcome."

"You'll make an excellent office manager, someday," Leslie said. "I think I put out all the fires. Half the staff called out and the other half is taking their place."

"And then everyone will be complaining next week the paychecks and tips are low and they can't pay their bills."

"Exactly. I don't get it, but some of them were legitimate excuses."

Leslie took the coffee to Tommy, careful not to put it on his desk near him. "Tommy? Tommy? Coffee."

He woke with a start, flailing his arms. When he saw her standing there, he grinned and wiped his eyes. "Thanks, dear. I musta fallen back out, see?"

"I see." Leslie checked her watch again. "We open in about an hour. My gut tells me we'll be busy." She handed him the coffee and he nodded in approval.

"Everything running smooth as silk?"

Leslie sighed. "As always. I have it under control."

"That's why they pay you the big bucks."

"I'll remember that next raise," she said.

"Call outs on a Saturday?"

"Of course. Why would anyone want to work and make big tips on a gorgeous day? You need to hire twenty more people so I can keep them in and out. I had half the staff call out today, but the other half is working. It's all good. Nothing your manager can't handle."

Tommy looked like he was about to say something else when her phone rang.

"Now what?" she said and smiled at Tommy. "We need to talk about that raise, sooner than later, boss. Hello?"

Tommy was watching her, with a bemused look on his face, as he sipped his coffee. She could only shake her head at him.

When she put the phone back in her pocket, she closed her eyes and sighed. "Do you have Greg's number handy?"

"Sure," Tommy said and chuckled. Greg was the kitchen manager, who was off today. He also covered Leslie when she had an emergency… like now.

"My daughter just totaled her car. She's not badly injured but is at the hospital."

Tommy waved her off. "I'll call Greg. You take care of your daughter."

Leslie smiled. "Good luck with your writing today. Thanks. I owe you one."

"I'll make a note of it for when you ask for your raise again, love."

Livin' It Up

Chrissie got her first table right at eleven, a two-top of locals. She knew them by name, only because the bartender, Woody, knew them. Heck, Woody knew everyone.

"Hi, ladies," she said with a smile.

Bethany and Colleen returned her smile, ignoring the menus handed to them. "Is Woody coming in today?"

Chrissie nodded. "He should have been in already. He's probably running late, as usual. You know Woody, fashionably late." Chrissie glanced back toward Tommy's office. If the boss or Leslie saw him slip in late again, they would be pissed.

"Yeah, we should have known better," Bethany said.

"What do you want to drink?"

Colleen glanced at the Tiki bar, where Woody would be working. "I think I'm going to wait until he comes in. He knows exactly what I want and how to make it."

"Not a problem," Chrissie said and then saw his pickup truck bullet into the parking lot next door. "I think he just pulled up, anyway. Can I start you with an appetizer?"

"Asian pot stickers and, also, chips and salsa," Bethany said, smiling when Woody came running across the street, trying not to be noticed. "Did he cut his hair?"

Chrissie was annoyed at the question and didn't know why. She barely talked to Woody, and knew many women came in just to flirt with him. As Leslie often said, he was good for business. The girls liked taking pictures with him and he knew everyone's name and what they drank. "Do you want me to give him your order?"

"Sure." Colleen and Bethany couldn't stop looking at him.

"Do you want to order anything else?"

"Nah, we'll start with the snacks and the drinks. We'll be here awhile," Bethany said without looking at her. "This is going to be a fun day."

* * * * *

"Those two?" Woody asked with a grin and waved at Bethany and Colleen from the Tiki bar. "Two strong Sharkbite drinks coming up. Start a tab for them, because they'll be here, staring at me, for hours."

Chrissie shook her head. "Do they ever say anything?"

"They flirt like mad and try to out-do the other one, but neither has ever gone past that. Every weekend, I can count on them being here." Woody pulled out a bottle of Captain Morgan rum, Blue Curacao, sour mix and Grenadine. "And, I can count on them drinking way too many of these. I give them the best one first but then, slowly, crank them down so they don't kill anyone. Someone usually shows up later and takes their keys, which is good, too."

"But never you?" Chrissie asked.

Woody shook his head. "Nope. Not interested."

"You're into dudes?"

Woody almost spilled his concoction, as he was mixing. "No, I am into women. Trust me. Just not those two."

Chrissie looked at the two women, both staring at Woody. "Why not? You could do a lot worse. They are both very pretty." Bethany was a dark-haired beauty with a glowing smile and curvy body, while Colleen had long blonde hair and an infectious laugh and quite a sizeable chest. Any guy would take either of them home.

"Oh, I agree." Woody glanced at them, as he put their drinks on the bar for Chrissie. "They just don't interest me. My thing is this: if I date a customer and it doesn't work out, we lose a customer or they keep coming in and it's weird. I already have a bad reputation, right?"

"No," Chrissie said, too quickly. Woody did have a bad rep among the staff and customers as being a bit of a player, but no one had a first-person story about sleeping or messing around with him. It was just… assumed he was lucky enough to have slept with women who didn't talk, or ones who were still sleeping with him. He was discreet, which drew even more women to him. And, Chrissie admitted, he was very handsome.

He waved her off. "I know what they say about me, and to be honest, I use it for my own advantage. No one really knows me. I could be into dudes or I could be married or I could be a million other things. I'm not just a cliché bartender who only lives to serve drinks and bang chicks on the beach or behind a dumpster after my shift. No one has ever gotten to know me, though."

Chrissie picked up the two Sharkbites and took a step away. "Thanks for the drinks," she said and turned her back to him. She didn't want to get further into this conversation with him. What if he was using lines on her? Pretending he was this reserved, emotional guy, who was misunderstood? This might be his way into a girl's pants, and Chrissie didn't want to find out the hard way.

*   *   *   *

"Why don't you go over and talk to him?" Bethany asked Colleen. "He keeps smiling at you."

"I think he's smiling at you."

"Really? You think so?" Bethany asked, staring at Woody. She thought he was looking at her but was trying to be nice to her friend. They'd known each other a long time, but each would step over the other for a chance with a good-looking guy. It was just a given and nothing personal. In all other facets of their lives, they were the best of friends but, when it came to men, all was fair in love and war. "Maybe after another drink or two."

"We do this every weekend, and neither of us ever talks to him. I'm going to do it," Colleen said and put her hands on the arms of the chair to stand up.

"Seriously?" Bethany asked, panic in her voice. What if Colleen did talk to him, and got with him because she was too scared to talk to Woody? They'd been coming to the Golden Lion for weeks, and Bethany thought she was safe in the fact Colleen was as scared as she was to talk to him. "I hope he really is looking at you."

Colleen hesitated. "Why would you say that?"

Bethany shrugged. "I'm just saying… if he liked either of us, he would come over and talk, right? Maybe he's just doing his job. Bartending is like being a stripper but keeping your clothes on. Talk to the losers and get their money."

"You calling me a loser?" Colleen asked, annoyed.

"If I'm calling you a loser, I'm also calling myself one. All I'm saying is, if he was interested, he would have said something already." As soon as Bethany heard her say this, she paused. She'd done it to keep Colleen from doing what she was too chicken-shit to do, but now she knew her words might be true. If Woody really wanted either of them, he had ample time to make his move. The guy had a reputation for being quite the ladies man, but he only smiled and waved at them.

Colleen got comfortable in her chair and gulped down her drink, looking around for Chrissie so she could get another. "Where's the food already?"

A handsome guy came out, carrying pot stickers and chips with salsa, smiling as he put them on the table. "Ladies," he said, quietly.

"Hi," Bethany said, pushing out her chest and grinning. "Who might you be?"

"I'm Andy. Chrissie asked me to run these out for you. Do you need anything else?"

Colleen grinned. "I see something I really want."

"Same," Bethany purred.

Andy looked confused but his smile didn't drop. "OK… um, well… if you need anything, let your waitress know."

"Why can't you be our waitress?" Bethany asked and then wanted to kick herself. "I mean, why can't you be our waiter?"

"We help each other out," he said and then walked away. Bethany stared at his butt and his broad shoulders through the tight Golden Lion Café shirt. "Yummy."

"He's too young for you," Colleen said.

"If that's the truth, he's too young for you, too."

Colleen grinned. "He's not that young, and I ain't that old."

"We're the same age."

"It's how you feel. I feel as old as he is. Whatever that is. As long as he's legal," Colleen said.

"Too funny. I hope he's into MILF's."

"So do I."

* * * * *

"You're really going to do this?" Colleen asked. They were into their fourth drink each, having eaten all the appetizers, and waiting for a fish and chips to share.

Bethany grinned. "Why not? What do I have to lose?"

Besides your dignity? "Nothing," Colleen said. "Just make sure he's into you, because, if he isn't, you'll blow it for us here. I like coming to Golden Lion and drinking. A screw-up and we'll be sitting at Johnny D's or Oceanside and having to start all over."

Bethany stopped smiling. "I never thought of that. Damn." She watched him as he strutted past their table to take an order. "He is really hot, and I haven't had someone as cute as him in way too long." She turned to Colleen. "I'm in my mid-forties and heading in the wrong direction. So are you. We need to live a little before we become old spinsters."

"You're being a bit dramatic, but I get what you are saying." Colleen thanked Chrissie when she put two plates down on their table and asked if they wanted another round. "Sure, why not."

"Suddenly, I'm feeling like an old fool and just want to have another drink and go home," Bethany said. "I think it's going to be an early day for me. I waste too many hours here, every Saturday, and I need to have a relaxing weekend before going back to work on Monday."

"I agree. One more drink and then we'll get going."

* * * * *

Bethany drove west on Route 100 and into Palm Coast, before punching the steering wheel in frustration. What was she thinking? She wasn't a quitter, and Colleen had psyched her out. Damn her.

She took a sharp right onto Colbert and spun her Mustang around, shooting through a yellow light and heading back east at breakneck speed. "I might go down in a blaze of glory, but I'm doing this on my terms," she said, as she checked her makeup in the rearview mirror. She might be running toward fifty but she looked damn good for her age, and men ten years younger often hit on her. Bethany hoped a guy as young as Andy would be interested.

In the short time since she'd left the Golden Lion parking lot, it had filled in. She parked a block down and made sure her cleavage was looking good and her lipstick was perfect, her short skirt waving in the breeze.

Woody, busy with the Tiki bar now two and three deep, looked confused and waved at her as she passed him. Bethany smiled and kept going, eyes peeled for Andy. She had no idea what she was going to say to him, but she wasn't deterred.

She caught a glimpse of him inside, exiting the kitchen, and swept to the front of the restaurant to cut him off as he moved near the steps leading to the upper deck. Bethany decided a direct approach would be the best. A simple hello and then ask him what time he got off work, and if he'd meet her for a drink.

As he came out, Bethany cocked a hand on her hip and stepped in his way just as Colleen came from the opposite side.

"Hi, ma'am… ma'am," Andy said, addressing both women before rushing past with a tray of food.

"What are you doing? I thought you left," Colleen said.

"I thought *you* left."

Both women moved closer, hands balled into fists.

"The plan was for us to get out of here and get on with our lives," Colleen spat. "You just agreed with me so you could get rid of me and come back."

"And you only said what you said so I'd leave. Pretty sneaky."

"You came back fast enough. I could say the same about you." Colleen glanced at Andy, who was heading back toward them. "What do we do now?"

"I'm asking him out," Bethany said. "Hi, Andy," she blurted as he tried to step around them. "What are you doing?"

He shrugged as he walked. "Working. I thought you ladies were gone already."

"Nope. Just hanging around," Colleen said.

Andy kept walking, disappearing inside the building.

Bethany and Colleen looked at each other and began laughing.

"What the heck are we doing?"

"I don't know, but I feel pretty stupid."

"So do I. I can't believe we did this."

"I'll see you next week?"

"Sure. Maybe we can embarrass ourselves in front of someone else then."

* * * * *

Andy smiled when the two women walked away, shaking his head at his luck. They were both old enough to be his mother, or at least too old for him. But it never failed.

"Wow, you seem popular with the geriatric crowd," Chrissie said, as she walked past. She stopped. "I'm kidding, they aren't that old. But it must be flattering to have women throw themselves at you."

"They never even got around to doing it, but they were talking pretty loud before they left yet again." Andy was waiting for Woody to complete his drink order.

"What's going on?" Woody asked.

"Bethany and Colleen both tried to ask Andy out," Chrissie said.

Andy tried to ignore the pissed look on Woody's face. He didn't want to cut into his action. He was the new kid on the block, and Woody was a legend in Flagler Beach. The last thing he wanted was to make enemies of this guy. "It's not a big deal. They didn't really say anything to me."

"They stuttered through, I heard them," Chrissie said and punched Andy lightly on the arm.

Woody slammed his drink order on the bar and sighed. "Here you go, kid." He turned away to help a line of customers.

Andy didn't like the attitude but couldn't do much about it. He wanted to keep his job, and knew the pecking order. He was at the bottom.

Chrissie smiled. "Don't let Woody bother you. He's probably just jealous because those two have been making googly eyes at him for weeks without saying a word. They see you and go all gaga."

Andy looked at Woody. "I don't want to get on his bad side."

"He doesn't have a bad side," Chrissie said. "He's got plenty of women throwing themselves at him. He won't lose sleep over it."

Andy liked Chrissie. She seemed like fun, and she was a pretty blonde. And… "What are you doing after work?" he asked.

Chrissie blushed but glanced in Woody's direction again. "Nothing. But I don't date people from work. Sorry."

"No, I just meant we could maybe hang out and get a drink or something," Andy said, quickly. Now he felt like an idiot.

Chrissie walked away but smiled over her shoulder. "Maybe."

Stories We Could Tell

Woody pulled his Cubs baseball cap down, the brim just touching his glasses. The sun was getting to him today, even with the roof of the Tiki bar blocking most of it and a nice breeze coming off the Atlantic Ocean. The Golden Lion Café was packed today and, even though they should just be getting through the initial noon rush, he could see the parking lot was filled and A1A parking was hard to come by.

Another perfect day in paradise.

"I need two Long Island Ice Teas, a Sundowner and a Jamaican Fizz," Amy said, as she passed by on her way to the kitchen.

"I'm a little busy here," Woody said with a grin.

"Not too busy for me, honey." Amy winked and kept moving.

"You're lucky you're so damn cute," Woody said.

"Amen to that," Carl, one of the regulars seated on a stool at the Tiki bar, said. He lifted his Budweiser and saluted Woody with it. "One time, I'll get her to look at me. I swear."

"Good luck, buddy. You gotta have faith, right?" A slick-haired man wearing designer sunglasses said from the other side of the bar. He'd been sipping on the same Corona for the last hour, feeding shots of Jack Daniels in between. Woody had offered to get him a cold beer but he'd declined. He had a slight accent Woody couldn't place, maybe English or Australian. Either way, he probably preferred his beer warm. Woody decided to think of him as Slick until he gave a name.

"I have faith… faith Crazy Amy will never give me the time of day," Carl said. Everyone crowded around the bar laughed.

"Don't call her that; she'll hate you even more," Woody said, as he began making her drink order. This was the part he loved: half a dozen drinks to make while keeping up on the customers surrounding him at the bar. "And she hates you enough already, I think."

"Dick," Carl said with a laugh. "You'll see. Someday I'll be in bed with Crazy Amy, and then you can all go to hell."

"I just hope she cleans up after Woody, or you'll be kissing her and knowing what he had for lunch," a woman Woody didn't recognize said, and the bar erupted with more laughter.

It didn't matter he'd never been with Amy. Of course, he'd never let on he wasn't the womanizer they all thought he was. He had a reputation to uphold. It was better they thought he was the lady killer in town and when he refused to kiss and tell, merely giving a wink and a smile, it did more for his rep than giving some lame story about banging the random customer.

"She's too nice a girl under all those tats, you know," Captain Rob said from his usual seat near the beer taps. He waved his empty beer glass. "But, she definitely likes the attention. I once had her and some dude in the back of *The Yellow Submarine*, and they were going at it hot and heavy."

"*The Yellow Submarine?*" Slick asked.

"My cab. I own the Magic Bus Cab Company," Captain Rob said. "She is a beauty and she is very flirty, but when she'd had enough she let him know it. That dude was halfway trying to unbutton his pants and get into hers when she told him no. She was just there to kiss and then get home. Driving the dude home was quite humorous to me, since he was so flustered and had no idea what hit him."

Woody filled Captain Rob's glass and slid it in front of the man. He liked Rob, one of those characters in town. He was usually seen driving his golf cart on the side streets or up and down A1A, waving at people like he was the mayor. Woody supposed he was to most of the locals and tourists, since he knew everyone and had given most a ride home from a drunken party night. He'd sit here and kill a few hours, and then be back in his cab, at the end of the night, to pick up one or two of the people he was drinking with.

Amy came out from the kitchen and walked, slowly, past the Tiki bar with a tray laden with food, a smirk on her face. "Are you boys talking about me again?"

"Nope," Carl said. Suddenly, the contents of his beer glass were more important than anything, and he buried his nose in it. "Not us."

"Ha." Amy smiled at Captain Rob. "Scouting your future fares?"

"Of course. I'm hoping Carl gets too drunk to drive and then too drunk to know I'm gouging him in *The Yellow Submarine*. It works for me. How else could I afford this beer?"

* * * * *

Slick finally ordered another Corona but let it sit in the hot sun while he downed three more shots of Jack, grimacing as he pounded them one after the other.

"Slow down there, buddy... this isn't the best weather to be sliding warm shots of Jack down your throat so quickly," Woody said.

Slick shrugged. "I need three more." He glanced over his shoulder at the parking lot. "Put them on my tab."

"Suit yourself." Woody stepped away from him and, slowly, got three more shots ready, watching the man. He didn't look inebriated, despite the multiple drinks. Woody decided to cut him off after this round, though. And his tab was beginning to build.

Rene came up and took the only empty seat, closest to the register. She was a striking blonde with a sexy tattoo running from her neck to the top of her foot on one side of her slim body, and she was always smiling.

"What can I get you today? Usual?"

Rene nodded and tapped her fingers on the bar. "You know it. I had a client this morning and now I can relax for the weekend. Heading up to Saint Augustine tonight to meet a guy."

Woody put the three shots in front of Slick and pulled a cold Coors Light from the case under the counter and popped the top. He placed it before Rene with a flourish. "You want an appetizer or are you just drinking?"

She seemed to be thinking about it before, finally, nodding. "Chips and salsa should hold me over. I hope this guy isn't going to take me to a drive-thru with coupons."

"You don't know where you're going?"

"Some Italian restaurant near the parking garage."

"You mean the seafood place? It's really good," Carl said, butting into the conversation, which he was apt to do.

Rene shrugged. "I thought it was a seafood restaurant but he said Italian. Either way… as long as he is as nice as my friend says."

Woody grinned. "Blind date? Really? In this day and age? Didn't you look him up on Facebook first? What if he's got a hunchback?"

"What if he has a lazy eye, bad teeth and a hideous scar?" Carl added.

Rene looked distraught, gripping her Coors Light. "My friend said he was really nice."

All the men at the Tiki bar groaned in unison.

"You know what guys say when we try to set up a buddy with an ugly chick so we can get with her hot friend? She has a great personality. You'll like her. She's nice."

Rene fumbled with her cell phone. "I need to get online and, at least, see a picture of him before I go."

"I would," Woody said, and grinned with all the guys at the bar. They were messing with her and having a laugh at her expense. Woody thought she was a great gal and many nights they'd sat here and talked about anything and everything, but he couldn't pass up an easy tease. "Of course, there's no guarantee his picture is updated. Some old dudes use their pictures from ten years ago, or their thirty year old son's photo. I knew a guy who took photos of good-looking guys and used them for his profile."

Rene closed her eyes. "I swear I will kill her if she set me up with some asshole."

"I'm sure you'll be fine. Just be late and when you see him standing in front of the restaurant and he's, like, eighty years old, pull away," Woody said.

Rene frantically pounded her thumbs over her phone and pulled the tiny screen closer to her face. "I think I found him."

"What's his name?" Carl asked.

"James Butcher."

Everyone around the Tiki bar groaned, again.

"Oh, no… what?" Rene asked, her voice rising.

Slick slapped the counter with his open palms. "James Butcher? Isn't it obvious? He's using the Fake Guy Name we all use." He looked around at the other men at the bar. "Am I right?"

"He's right. We've all used it, and we all have the password to the fake profiles on the computer, too. He could be anyone, but he isn't the guy in the picture. That's a guarantee," Woody said. He was starting to enjoy this, even though it was cruel and Rene was going to punch someone.

"Damn." She put her phone as close to her face as she could without her nose touching it. "He's actually cute. Older than me, with a ponytail and a warm smile. He's dressed all Jimmy Buffett and, in his other pictures, he's on a Harley." Rene looked up and frowned. "He has a bunch of pictures, and he looks normal."

"You've been duped," Carl said.

"He has a really great smile," Rene nearly whispered. "I need another Coors Light."

Woody pulled another beer out. "This one is on me."

"I don't want your pity," Rene said, as she put her phone back in her pocket.

"Oh, it's not pity. I just don't want you to kill me when you find out we are totally messing with you."

"What?"

Everyone around the bar began to laugh.

Rene gave Woody the finger, then moved her hand and let it linger, pointed at each person around the bar. "I, seriously, hate every one of you. If this guy turns out to be a creep, I will hunt all of you down."

* * * * *

"How about another beer, barkeep?" Slick asked.

"You got it," Woody said, glad he hadn't ordered three more shots. The guy had, barely, finished his last beer after another hour and he'd nurse this one. "I'll add it to your tab."

"Much obliged."

There was something *off* with Slick. Woody had been a bartender long enough to be able to read people, and the guy's body language alone was enough for concern. He was trying to remain casual but he watched every person entering and exiting the Golden Lion, his eyes darting and reading each customer. He was waiting for something or someone. Slick had angled his chair to be able to see both exits and the side street, as well.

Woody knew, instinctively, he wasn't just checking out the hot women and wasn't waiting for a lunch date. This guy was tense, and whoever, finally, showed wouldn't be someone Slick wanted to meet, even in a public place.

He'd briefly joined in when they were teasing Rene but then had gone quiet again, preferring to stare at the parking lot and the upper deck, eyes shifting back to the front bar and the A1A entrance.

Slick took two sips of his Corona and wiped the condensation with his hand, rubbing the cool water onto the back of his neck. "I don't suppose you'd set me up with three more shots?"

Woody smiled and slowly shook his head. "I'm not sure it would be a good idea, do you suppose?"

"I suppose it wouldn't, but I could use another round right now."

"Troubles?" Woody casually asked, doing his best aww-shucks bartender routine by pulling out his bar rag and wiping a phantom stain near Slick.

"You could say that."

"Well, sorry to hear. But, I think I'm going to have to ease you off the many shots you've had. We can't have you drunk out there in public, can we?"

Slick shrugged his shoulders. "I'm not driving out of here. I might walk, or be escorted."

Woody didn't like the sound of that. Was it a threat? "I'd hate to see you dragged out of here. It wouldn't be fun for anyone."

Slick stared across A1A at the Atlantic Ocean. "You ever go swimming in the water?"

"Of course. Some nights, after a long day here, I take off my shirt and shoes and run across the street and down the beach and jump in. It's so refreshing. It cools me off, gives me a second wind, and then I can begin my own fun at night."

"I should try it."

"Maybe you should." Woody eyed his warming beer. "Finish the Corona, pay your tab, and take a plunge."

Slick grinned. "You're afraid I'm going to bolt out of here before I pay for my ten shots."

"Fifteen shots."

Slick laughed. "And don't forget the beers." He stood and pulled out a wad of cash. "I'll take another shot of Jack for the road, if you don't mind. I'm not drunk, as you can clearly see from me standing, and I'm not driving out of here." Slick took another long look at the ocean. "Close me out and I'll give up my seat to the next man with a tale to tell."

"What tale is that?" Woody had to ask. Now he was curious. "And I can't seem to place your accent."

"I don't have an accent; you do."

Woody went to the register but kept one eye on Slick. If the guy was going to bolt, Woody could easily alert the staff. On the rare occasion someone tried to skip without paying, they were detained until the police showed. He needed to keep Slick talking until the bill was paid. "I guess we'll agree to disagree on the accent. What's your unique tale? Everyone who sits in that seat thinks their story is the distinctive one I haven't heard in my many years behind this bar."

"Have you ever heard one that was truly original?"

"My first three hours on the job. After that..." Woody trailed away with a smile. He printed out the receipt for the alcohol and put it in front of Slick.

Slick ignored the bill and sucked on his Corona. He put the bottle down and tapped on the counter. "Did you forget to include my last shot?"

"Not a chance. It's in there. I didn't add my generous tip, though."

"Good man." Slick was still holding the wad of cash. "Let me ask you a question before I pay."

Woody stretched. "I already know the answer. You'll outrun me but you won't outrun the two bouncers who I gave a signal to. You might even get into your car and get out of Flagler Beach, but you'll get pulled over. And for what? Less than a hundred bucks in beer and shots? That doesn't make much sense."

"I suppose not." Slick finished his beer and sat back down. He tossed five twenty dollar bills on the bar. "I'll be having my last shot and going, then."

Woody scooped up the money and went back to the register. "You never told me your story."

Slick was staring at the parking lot.

Woody followed his gaze to see a police cruiser as it parked at the far end of the lot and two officers exited the vehicle. "I'm going to guess this isn't a coincidence."

"Not a chance." Slick stood up. "You owe me for a shot."

"What's your story?"

"You'll read about it in the paper tomorrow."

"Not good enough. I want your version," Woody said, trying to stall the guy. If he'd done something really bad, Woody didn't want to see him escape, but didn't want to interfere in the event this guy was really bad.

"Ever here the song 'Bartender (Sittin' at a Bar)?"

"By Rehab. Of course. That you?"

Slick started walking to the front of the Golden Lion Café's exit. "Pretty much. But she bought me my last day of drinking and freedom, so she wasn't all that bad."

"You know you won't get far," Woody yelled after him.

The police must have seen him because one ran through the outside area of the restaurant and the other along the sidewalk to the front.

Everyone from the Tiki bar, who'd been sitting quietly and listening to Woody and Slick's exchange, got up and ran to A1A. Woody sighed and began cleaning up the empties and using the time to cut some limes and oranges and call for an order of beer to fill the coolers.

Carl was the first to return, ordering another beer before he even sat down on his stool. "You missed a good one."

"Did they tackle him in the street?"

"Nope. Crazy bastard ran into the ocean with his clothes on and started doing a backstroke."

"The cops chase him in?"

"Nah. They're still watching him."

"He's still in the water?"

Carl laughed. "In his shoes, and the wad of cash he put back in his pocket is all wet now."

When Austin came out with two cases of beer to refill the cooler, Woody slapped him on the back. "Man the bar; I'll be right back."

"No way."

Woody was already running to the stairs, heading up to the top deck. He joined everyone at the rail as word spread.

"He is a crazy bastard," Woody whispered.

Slick was now doing a doggy paddle, about a hundred feet off the shore, and heading north, at a slow pace. The police were, calmly, shouting from the beach for him to surrender and get out of the water. It wasn't working.

Woody went back to the Tiki bar, where Austin was leaning on the counter chatting with Carl and a few more regulars who'd decided the fun was over for them.

"Thanks," Woody said and watched Austin go back inside the restaurant.

"You gotta love this place," Carl said and tipped back a fresh beer.

Woody had to agree.

False Echoes

Creighton Northgate, known to his few friends as Crate, ordered another Budweiser, because it was the happy hour special. It didn't matter what the drink was, as long as it was cheap. His original idea was to buy a six-pack of something and settle into the hotel, but his room wasn't ready. So he'd driven his pickup truck up A1A until he'd seen the inviting sign for Golden Lion Café.

He'd meet with his new clients tonight after dinner, but for now he settled on finishing a few beers with the few bucks he had in his pocket. He usually worked further north than Florida, but he'd take a job wherever he could find it. Or the job found him.

"Another beer?"

Crate looked up from his corner table and tried to smile at the pretty young blonde asking the question. He idly scratched at the stubble on his face; he'd need to shave when he got to the room later so he'd look presentable. "I suppose I'll have to since you're twisting my arm."

She laughed and moved off, leaving Crate to down the last sip of beer. He was getting hungry but only had enough cash for alcohol. If the new client wanted to take him to dinner, he wouldn't discourage it. There was a dented can of Pringles in the truck he'd feast on, if he had to. And he'd need a six pack of beer in order to sleep tonight.

The air was hot but there was a nice breeze coming off the ocean. He was used to the weather in the south, but he was still getting sweaty. Crate needed a nice cold shower after driving for the last couple of days to get here. He still didn't know what the job was. He usually got a rough idea in some cases, and he'd interview important people tonight and fill in the blanks.

"Mind if I join you?"

Crate looked up as a tall brunette, with prominent cleavage showing, stood near his table, one hand on the chair across from him. She was stunning, and when she smiled Crate couldn't help but return it.

"Yes? No?" she asked, her voice just above a whisper.

The waitress came back and put another beer in front of Crate, taking the empty.

"Wait..." Crate turned to the brunette. "Do you want a drink?"

"No, thanks. Just a seat."

"Sure, of course," Crate said. He turned to the waitress, who was giving him a strange look. "Nothing else."

"Um, ok," she said and left, quickly, with his empty.

As soon as the brunette sat down, Crate frowned. "You're not..."

"No, I'm not. You of all people should know, and I'm surprised you didn't see it right away."

"You caught me off guard." Crate took a long pull from his beer. He watched as she folded her hands in her lap. She was wearing a stunning orange dress with matching stiletto heels, as if she was coming from or going to a formal engagement. "What brings you here?"

"The beach. I've always loved it here, even as a child. You?"

"Someone like you, I imagine," Crate said. "I go wherever this line of work takes me."

"Do you earn a good living with it?"

Crate held up his beer. "I can afford the cheapest happy hour beers and, pretty much, nothing else. It's not as glamorous as you'd think."

"I didn't think it was. At all. I can imagine the pain and the torment you must go through on a daily basis."

"Nothing a six-pack of beer can't cure every night." Crate scratched at his new beard again. "I'm just trying to get through life."

She snorted. "Is that supposed to be funny?"

Crate shrugged. "It is what it is. I find anyone I encounter in my, um, life, has their own propensity for things I say and do. I can't change everyone and I don't want to. I just want to do the things I need to do."

"You're so cryptic."

"Some folks don't like to hear what I have to tell them, you know. They're in denial."

"I was for years." She offered a lithe hand. "I'm Julie Malone, by the way. Pleased to meet you."

He didn't bother playing the game, his hand back to his beer. "Crate."

"That's an odd name."

"I suppose. Creighton, actually."

"I figured no parent, no matter how strange, would name their kid Crate." Julie laughed. "Maybe Barrel. Or Box."

"Then I guess I'm lucky to be called Crate."

"How's your Budweiser?" she asked, after an uncomfortable moment of silence. "I can't remember the last time I had a drink."

"Did you have a problem with alcohol?"

Julie nodded, with a smile, showing off perfect white teeth. "My problem was every guy at the Tiki bar would buy me a shot or a beer in hopes I'd loosen up. Silly boys and, occasionally, women."

"Interesting."

"Which part? The free drinks or the women hitting on me?"

Crate looked away but he couldn't help but smile. "I am, after all, only a man."

"An interesting one at that, Crate. Most of the customers and staff around here bore me, but I knew when you sat down, you were different, somehow. Why are you so different?"

"It's a long story, and I don't feel like sharing it right now." Crate looked around at the people eating at adjacent tables but no one was paying any attention to him. The story of his life. "I'm guessing you have a unique story."

"Don't we all, when it comes right down to it? My tale of woe might be interesting to some, but, to others, they've heard it all before. I've eavesdropped on so many tall tales at the Golden Lion over the years, they all run into one another. A few of them might even be true."

"Stranger things have happened."

"That's funny coming from you. I can tell."

Crate grew quiet when the waitress approached him again, almost cautiously. "Another beer?"

Crate nodded and held up a finger, slugging the last of the beer in front of him before handing her the empty. He was getting precariously low on funds but knew he needed at least one more to settle his nerves. Food would've been good, but that ship had already sailed, as far as his money was concerned.

"So, Crate, tell me where you've been lately."

Crate watched the waitress walk back inside the restaurant before turning back to Julie. "I've been everywhere. Simple as that. I never stop to think of where I've been, because I'm too busy trying to get where I'm going. You?"

"I was actually born in Chicago. I moved to Florida when I was six. No one was actually born in Florida, don't you know? It's just populated with northerners escaping the snow. From your accent, I know you weren't born this far south."

"Nope," was all Crate would give her. He was already growing tired with the beer, the heat and the sun, and this conversation. He needed to get in his pickup and see if his room was ready. "It was a pleasure meeting you. Good luck."

Julie laughed loudly, and Crate looked around, instinctively, to see if anyone had noticed. No one looked in their direction.

His last beer was set on the table without a word by the waitress and he, eagerly, drank from it, hoping to finish it off quickly so he could go.

"Are you suddenly in a hurry to get away from me?" Julie asked, annoyance clearly in her tone. "I finally get someone to talk to, and you're running away."

"I have work to do, and I need to rest up."

"What if I was your work? Wouldn't that be ironic?"

"Not really." Crate took another chug of beer. "You'd be surprised how many times it's happened. More often than not, lately. Like I'm a magnet for problems. Most of the time, I roll into town and someone like you gets in touch with me before the one's who are paying me. It tends to make it easy."

"Is it ever just a coincidence?"

"Of course. I never rule anything out. I just simply go through the motions. Sometimes we'll say good bye and I'll never see you again, and other times I'll be back in a few hours to sort out the mess you, or someone else, created."

"I'm the mess. Quite literally," Julie said, all bravado gone. "I've been here for too long."

"Some folks never want to leave, you know. The unknown is what scares them to stay in place, day in and day out. People don't like change, even if it can help them long-term. Sometimes it's unfinished business, sometimes it's living a dream, and sometimes it's just the fact no good deed goes unpunished. Who can say?"

Julie looked around, her eyes clearly tracing each contour of the ceiling above and the many quirky signs and color bursts. "I was here when this place opened. It was twenty years ago. It was a tiny little shack, really. Nothing like the gorgeous place it is now. There wasn't much more than the original frame of the main bar. Where we're sitting was sand and sea shells. Tommy has really built this place up over time. I've watched him. He's been a good owner and a good boss to these kids as they come and go, and his smile as gotten bigger as the gray has taken over his hair."

"That sounds wonderful." Crate looked around for the waitress. He needed his check and to hit the road. Now. "I wish you the best of luck."

"I was in my late twenties and we were heading to Saint Augustine when James and I stopped here to see what the commotion was." Julie stood and moved her hands around her dress. "He bought me this dress, and said I was the prettiest woman he'd ever met. I believed him in that moment. I believed him all through dinner when he couldn't stop staring at me. It was only our third date, and he was rich. He drove a fancy car, had expensive jewelry and a gorgeous smile."

Crate dropped all the cash he had on the table and stood up. "It was a pleasure meeting you."

"We took a walk on the beach," Julie continued. "Under the pier, he kissed me. He wanted more, but it was only our third date. I fought with him."

Crate sat back down and sighed. Why did everyone assume he had nothing better to do than solve the world's problems? And without compensation. He wasn't a bad guy. He was just tired. He had work to do tonight. And he needed a shower and a nap.

Julie leaned across the table and showed her perfect white teeth again, but this time it was more of a snarl, her lips thin and bloodless. "Can I show you where my body can be found?"

* * * * *

The police officer looked, skeptically, at Crate, sitting on the rail of the pier. "You say you just happened to be crawling under the boardwalk and found a bone?"

"A femur."

"You're not from around here," the cop added.

"Who really is? We're all transplants," Crate said and smiled. "I'm just passing through."

The officer stared at Crate's license again before handing it back. "Why does your name sound familiar?"

"I'm not sure," Crate said slowly. This didn't sound good.

The officer went to his cruiser and got on the radio. "Cherie, can you let Mayor Malone know I have a guy named Creighton Northgate at the pier. He's the one who found the bones. I remember the chief and the mayor mentioning this guy recently. It can't be coincidence."

"Nothing is coincidence," Crate muttered. He supposed he wouldn't be getting a nap, but, then again, he knew he'd already done his work in Flagler Beach.

He walked up to the officer. "The woman buried under the pier is Julie Malone. You might want to find out where a James Butcher is at this moment, because he's the killer."

"How could you possibly know this?"

Crate sighed. "Mayor Malone will explain it to you."

I Love The Now

Even without her skates and Palm Coast Roller Derby outfit on, many people in the inside eating area of the Golden Lion Café recognized Amber. She'd been in town for a number of years, and her red hair and easy smile won over many locals, even if they didn't fully understand what she did.

She was a roller derby girl, and she was quite proud of it. Her entire life was devoted to the team, and promoting the sport and the other girls she was sisters with. They practiced three nights a week at either the Youth Center in Palm Coast or at the Skate & Shake in nearby Ormond Beach, and had two bouts a month, as well as impromptu practices, trail skating on weekends when they weren't scrimmaging, and endless hours of getting the word out about the team.

Today, Amber was mixing business with pleasure. She was here to meet a neighbor for a late lunch and also to hand out some flyers for their upcoming bout. Most of the girls on the team took the promoting seriously, and they were constantly talking and plugging any bout coming up and inviting people to come to a practice. Especially other women. It was important to get new blood into the game, and they dubbed these new recruits Fresh Meat.

"Hey, Jenna," Amber said when she spotted her friend. She made her way to the table, smiling and waving at a few people who recognized her.

Jenna stood, awkwardly, and smiled. "I already ordered chips and salsa. I hope you don't mind."

"Not at all." Amber looked at Jenna, who was wearing tight black shorts and a loose yellow t-shirt. The angry red of a new tattoo was etched on her right calf. "More ink?"

Jenna laughed. "Jared and I are addicted now."

"Another Bible verse?"

"Isaiah 53:5. *By his stripes, we are healed.*"

"Pretty soon I won't have to read the Bible; you and your husband will have every important passage as a tattoo."

"That is the goal."

The waitress, Chrissie, came over with their appetizer and a sweet tea for Jenna. "What can I get you, Amber?"

"A sweet tea sounds really good. Is Tommy around?"

"He's in his office. You need him?"

Amber handed her four flyers. "Can you ask him or Leslie to hang these for me? It always helps."

"Not a problem."

"I'm going to make the offer again, you know," Amber said.

"No thanks. I'm not into getting knocked around and I can barely roller skate. I haven't been on wheels since I was nine. I like being in the crowd with a hot dog and a Coke and living vicariously through each check and fall. You couldn't pay me enough to get out there."

"If you ever change your mind, or want to come out for the recruiting next week, let me know. I think you'd be dynamite. You have the look and the attitude. We can teach you the game, and how to skate. Heck, we have girls who came to us and had never skated before. They are some of our best teammates now. Think about it."

"I will."

Amber turned back to Jenna. "How's J and J Fitness doing?"

"Awesome," Jenna said proudly. She and her husband, Jared, owned the fitness training center on the corner of Moody Avenue and North Flagler Avenue. The two had been through some trials and tribulations over the years, but just when it looked like they'd be down, out and forgotten, they found Faith. And a renewal in their religious beliefs and one another. They devoted themselves to, not only The Lord, but to being better people. Amber loved Jenna, and her positive vibes always rubbed off on Amber and did wonders for her attitude for days. "You should really come by tomorrow morning. A good workout would help."

"I already work out too much with the roller skating. These thick legs get enough pounding. I can't imagine getting up that early, either."

"It's not *that* early."

"What time do you start?"

Jenna smiled. "Five a.m. We do a prayer group. You don't have to come to it, but the session lasts an hour and gets you in the right frame of mind to do anything. It's very inspiring. If you shy away from the religious aspect, come over at six. We begin what we call the Boot Camp, and it will test your body. I love it."

"You're a skinny thing, of course you love it," Amber said. "I weigh twice as much as you."

"All I hear is an excuse. I weighed more than you a couple of years ago, and you know it. All I did was sit on my fat butt, drinking, and eating junk food while Jared and I tried to get through another painful day. We didn't practice what we preached. Now we do, body and mind. It doesn't have to take a scare to get you motivated." Jenna smiled. "Sometimes a caring neighbor gets you going. The Boot Camp is free, so it's not a money excuse."

"Maybe."

Jenna leaned forward and put a hand on Amber's arm.

"Stop looking at me with your dimples," Amber said. Jenna had such a pretty, warm face, and, when she smiled, she lit up. Like now. "I'll be there. Six in the morning on a Sunday. You're killing me."

"Excellent. Reba has been going, as well."

"Not to the five a.m., I don't imagine."

Jenna laughed. "No, she shows up at six and gets her workout in. She has so much nervous energy. She's a riot to see trying to keep up and attempting to do better than everyone else."

Reba Port was the neighbor who lived between them, and she was a stay at home mom with twins. Her husband, Sam, ran a software company out of his home office, so the Ports were usually home. Reba often talked about trying to be a successful author in her own right, but so far no one had read any of her work. She could sometimes be found sitting in Kokomo's Café, with a cooling cup of coffee, while she pounded away on her laptop, or sitting in Veteran's Park and daydreaming.

Tommy came out, and he smiled at the two women. "How's it going, uh? Enjoying the gorgeous weather?"

"You can't beat it. I brought some flyers for the roller derby," Amber said. "I hope you can put them up for us."

"I'd love to. You roller derby ladies crack me up, you know."

"How so?" Jenna asked.

Tommy smiled and sat down at the table. "They all come across as big, tough ladies when they're out there havin' their bout and whatnot, but I see them in here all dolled up with their kids and families and they are some of the sweetest people I know." Tommy wagged a finger. "But get them riled up with a pair of skates on and I've seen them knock another girl across the rink with a flick of their hips. Amazing, really."

Amber turned to Jenna. "It is a lot of fun."

"I imagine not when you're getting knocked around," Jenna said.

"Are you going to try out for the team? Brilliant," Tommy exclaimed. "I think you'd be a natural."

"Why?" Jenna asked.

Tommy grinned and spread his hands. "You've got a beautiful look, love, and the tattoos and the attitude are wonderful. I used to watch roller derby in the sixties, and it was always fascinating. I need to get out to a bout, huh? When's the next one?"

It was Amber's turn to smile. "I gave you the flyer."

Tommy poked himself in the head playfully. "Right, right. My brain's a bit addled at times. I got this novel in me head trying to get out. I can't seem to write it down fast enough some days."

"What are you writing about?"

Tommy leaned back in the chair and looked embarrassed. "I'm not sure if it's anything good, see? Just something my head cooked up one day. I once wrote a song about Jimmy Buffett, and from the lyrics came the story. It's about a man who goes out into the world in search of adventure, really. I guess that sums it up, but it's not finished. I'm really, really close to being done. Maybe this week…" He looked off at the ocean and his voice dropped to a whisper. "I've been writing it for years. Every few days I get a burst of inspiration. A few more lines, another page and another chapter complete."

"Sounds great. I can't wait to buy a copy of it in the bookstore," Amber said.

Tommy shrugged. "Maybe you can buy it at the gift shop here, or in Flagler Gift Shop or Bahama Mama's. They've all already said they would sell it for me, but I guess I need to finish it and get someone to rip it apart. Get a publisher or just go ahead and do it myself like you see the local authors doing all the time."

"Good luck with it. You just need to stay focused and positive. You'll get there," Jenna said.

"You lovely ladies have a great day and enjoy. I'll get the flyers up right now," Tommy said, before giving them both a pat on the arm and leaving.

"Now, where were we?" Amber asked.

"You were coming out tomorrow morning to Boot Camp, and I was going to whip you into even better shape for roller derby."

"Yes, you're right." When Jenna smiled, Amber tapped her fingers on the table. "Of course, it then means you're going to come out this week and try out for the roller derby team."

"That's not fair."

"Life isn't fair. I'm willing to sacrifice my big ass and sweating and cursing you, so you have to do the same thing. I'm sure there's a Scripture quote on you somewhere about it."

Jenna stopped halfway to dipping a chip in the salsa. "That's not fair. You can't use my faith against me. I could point out three of them, but I refuse to be baited by you."

"It's just as well, I guess," Amber said.

Jenna put the chip in her mouth and looked away.

"It's just as well," Amber repeated.

"Nope. I'm not going to be baited. Forget it."

Amber sat back in her chair and put her hand on her chin in a thoughtful pose, squinting one eye.

Jenna glanced over at her and looked away again. "The ocean is beautiful. I wonder how cold it is."

"You really don't seem like the roller derby type, anyway. You're too soft."

"It's not working."

"Look at your short arms, too... and those legs."

Jenna turned back to Amber. "What about my legs?"

"Nothing. They're just short, and don't look too powerful anyway. Like sticks. Toothpicks. They'd snap at the first check. Good thing you're chickening out."

"You can't trick me. And I don't have toothpick legs."

"Toothpick Legs might be your roller derby name. It fits. I'm just glad I won't have to babysit you in a bout so you don't get hurt."

"Not funny."

"You also look like you have a low threshold for pain. Am I right? I'm sure you cry when you break a nail, or stub your toe. There's no crying in roller derby."

"There's no crying in baseball," Jenna said.

"There, either. The other team would make fun of you, and I'm sure Jared would rush onto the track and hand you a tissue."

"Now you're just being annoying."

"Not even close. I have plenty more to go."

"Fine."

"Fine what?"

Jenna sighed. "Fine as in I'll go. Just tell me where and when. But you need to leave me alone until then."

"I can't promise you that, and I think you know it. How about this: I bust your chops a little bit each day until you and the rest of the Fresh Meat strap on the skates."

"Fresh Meat? I don't like the sound of that, you know."

Amber shrugged. "Live with it. We've all been there and proven ourselves. You can't just join the team; you have to earn it. That way it makes it special when/if you finally make it, and get to bout with us against other teams."

"OK. I'm in." Jenna smiled. "Suddenly, I see so many possibilities for tomorrow's Boot Camp with you."

Amber smiled. "Remember… I can give as much as I get, so watch yourself."

Jenna clapped. "This is going to be fun."

Smart Woman (In A Real Short Skirt)

She pretended not to notice the two guys staring at her from across the Tiki bar, as she sat calmly sipping her Corona and digging into the peanuts on display in front of her.

The older guy to her left kept trying to get a good look down her thin cut-off t-shirt, but Tosha Shorb kept moving her shoulder slightly to block his view and tease him a bit. "Somebody in this place better buy me a drink," she whispered and took another mouthful of beer. She wanted mixed drinks, dinner and dancing. She was restless and she'd only been in Florida for about eight hours.

Her long curly red hair was flowing over her shoulders, but she was starting to rethink sexy versus sweaty. If she moved slightly to her right, a beam of sunlight would drop onto her fair shoulders, and she'd be fried in half an hour. With her super tight white skirt and her white g-string riding up her butt crack, she didn't have much skin covered. Her twin sister had offered to slather sunscreen on her but she declined. Tosha didn't want to smell like a tourist, and, if she did it right, she'd have some color by the end of the day.

"The bathroom is really cool," her sister, Trista, said. "Really Florida funky like I imagined it. I wanted to just hang out in there but I got thirsty." She sat down on the bar stool to the right of Tosha, directly in the sun, but her giant straw hat, oversized sunglasses and gobs of sun block still caked to her nose and cheeks blocked every last centimeter of harmful rays from penetrating her outfit.

"You're embarrassing in that getup, you know," Tosha said and took another drink.

Trista ordered a diet soda, even though both girls were curvy but skinny. While they were twins and shared some basic features, they were like night and day. Tosha preferred being the extrovert, the loud party girl having fun, and her sister was a shut-in who only dealt with others in video games. She preferred to be called Mathyu, after her main character. Tosha refused to call her some stupid name that made no sense.

"What do you want to do today?" Tosha asked. She was getting bored sitting here in the heat, and, so far, a few guys had smiled at her but no one had bought her a drink. Back home in Pennsylvania, dudes would have flocked to her in a club or bar, trying to get with the redhead and see if the curtains matched the carpet. Not many guys got to see the real answer: bare floors.

"I say we eat some crazy Florida food and then go back to the hotel. I need to be online soon. I have the WoW tournament coming up tonight and I want to get together with my team and discuss strategy."

"Why not call them on an actual phone?"

Trista shook her head and gave her twin her best condescending look. "We don't talk on the phone. We talk through our headsets and in the game. Why would I call someone? One of the team members, Raffi, lives in Germany. You know how much it would cost to call Germany?"

"You could Skype him."

"He's a she, and Skype is for twelve year old girls."

"And basing your life around video games, even while on vacation, isn't?"

Trista laughed. "No way. Everyone plays video games. Even you."

"Not as crazy as you do. I like to play for the enjoyment and to see if I can kill things and kill time. You use it as your only social interface. It's sad, if you think about it."

"I don't think about it." Trista sipped her soda. "All I think about is the next mission, and staying alive."

"Spoken like a true warrior."

Trista smiled. "Wow, thank you."

"Ugh. That was sarcasm, sis. Over your head yet again."

"I take it as a compliment."

"You would."

"I did."

Tosha decided she needed to go to the bathroom. "I'll be right back. Don't do anything goofy while I'm gone."

"What? Me?" Trista said. She pulled out the tube of sunscreen from her oversized beach bag. "I'll just dab more on while you're gone."

"No," Tosha said and sighed. "That would be listed under goofy things to do."

"I'm not going to burn in this sun. I have fair skin." Trista pinched her sister's arm. "We have fair skin, sis. You should cover up or you'll be burnt to a crisp. We redheads fry like bacon in this sun. This isn't Pennsylvania."

"It's the same damn sun."

"Not even close. We are a thousand miles closer to the equator. I can already see how red your shoulders are getting. I guarantee by tonight you'll be crying like a baby."

"I can guarantee I'll be moaning tonight, and it won't be from sunburn. It will be from some young Florida son hammering this tourist."

Trista wrinkled her nose. "Why do you say stuff like that?"

"Because I know it annoys you. And it makes me laugh."

* * * * *

"I'm going to follow her," Chazz said, as he watched from across the Tiki bar as the gorgeous redhead get off her stool. "She kept looking at me."

"Um… no she didn't. She was probably pissed you kept drooling in her direction," Marco said. "Why can't you calm down and help me look for Chelle?"

Chazz laughed at his friend. "You mean Michelle."

"Asshole." Marco turned in his chair and began scanning the parking lot across the street for the tenth time in the last hour.

Michelle - Chelle - was a girl Marco had briefly encountered yesterday when they first came to the Golden Lion Café, and he was quite smitten with her. Despite the fact she'd completely blown him off and left without even looking at him, Marco had spent the night looking for her in and out of the bars in Flagler Beach.

"Dude, she isn't going to come to the same place for lunch two days in a row. Who does that? Nobody, except in bad John Cusack movies."

"There's no such thing as a bad John Cusack movie." Marco turned to Chazz. "I'm telling you, she'll be here."

"I'll bet you a hundred bucks she doesn't show."

"I'll take your money."

"You're a sucker. I'm going to follow Red to the bathroom and get her phone number. These Florida chicks are easy."

Marco snorted. "You've been here almost two days and not one has even looked at you."

"Those strippers did yesterday."

"You bought them drinks and gave them money. Of course they did, stupid."

"Buy me another beer. I'll be right back." Chazz casually pointed across the bar. "Why don't you go over and talk up her friend while I'm busy? You'll be banging the plain one while I get the wild redhead."

"They're both redheads, you moron. And they look like twins."

"Not from where I'm standing."

"Seriously, I think they are twins."

Chazz shook his head and squinted at the other woman who'd been sitting with the hot chick. There was no way they were related. This girl had the same color hair but it was jammed into a stupid giant beach hat, and her body was covered up. She wasn't showing off her curves like the other one. Marco was nuts. "I'm wasting time," Chazz finally said. "She'll be done taking a piss before I move."

"Don't think I'm going to do something stupid for you, dude. I have my own agenda for being back in this place."

Chazz ignored his friend's comment. Ever since yesterday and seeing the big blonde, it was all Marco would talk about, and it was starting to get annoying. Shit, he was crazy talking about staying in Florida and Flagler Beach just so he could get to know her. Chazz would never get him. Back in New Jersey, Marco Petrucci had his pick of the litter, and the women loved him. He was a smart, good-looking guy who worked for Chenzo and the mob behind the scenes, their main computer hacker. Gone were the days of hit men and colorful nicknames, replaced by a steel efficiency when it came to crime. And as much as Chazz fancied himself a mobster, he was only in the loop because he was a blood relative of the bigwigs above him, and he knew it. And he was comfortable knowing he had that power above and protecting him.

Marco was a rare commodity, though: a smart guy who kept his mouth shut and his nose clean, didn't get caught up in drama or drugs, and did a lot for the Family when it came to computer hacking, online banking and money laundering, and getting the jump on the Feds and anyone else who was watching them. And there were many eyes turned on them at any given moment. Chazz thought his best friend was delusional for thinking he could walk away from his job, but figured they'd enjoy the vacation in Florida, the blonde would never be found, and they could return to Newark and their normal lives.

The redhead was coming out of the women's restroom when Chazz walked up, putting on his sexiest smile and acting casual. As she walked past him, she returned his grin with a nod.

Chazz lightly reached out and touched her arm. "Hey, how's it going?"

She stopped. "Good. You?"

"Excellent now." He made sure he kept eye contact. He'd learned the move from Marco. Show your dominance by locking their gaze and letting them look away first.

"Good to hear."

She wasn't looking away. She had a pretty face and nice skin, her red hair cascading over her slender shoulders, but she had a powerful build as well. Chazz noticed with delight she had pert little breasts, and her hips were curvy.

"Are you done with your inventory?" she asked.

Chazz locked eyes again but now her look was intense, no hint of humor in them. "Um, yeah, I mean sorry. You are so good-looking, I couldn't help myself. I'm sure you get that all the time."

"I do." Now she leaned in closer, her nose scrunched up. "Are you from Jersey?"

Chazz smiled. "Yes, I am. How can you tell?"

"The annoying accent." She crossed her arms. "I'm from Harrisburg."

"Pennsylvania girl? How cool is that? It's like fate brought us here."

"Or an airplane."

Chazz had no response. She hadn't really given him a great line to build on, but he decided to push ahead. "How long are you and that other chick here for?"

"That other chick is my twin. We're here for a few days."

"Cool. Really cool."

She laughed. "Well-said. Those Jersey school systems are amazing."

"Yeah." Chazz had nothing.

"Well, it was great wasting four minutes talking about nothing with you, but I need to get back to my twin before my head explodes. Good luck with whatever you think you're doing in Florida, buddy."

"Wait, before you go… why don't the four of us hang out tonight? Dinner and then a walk on the beach."

Now she was really laughing. "Do you think I came down to Florida to find some lame Jersey boyfriend? I came to meet a young Florida dude and have a wild weekend so I could go back to PA and never have to see or talk to him again."

"Just give me a chance," Chazz said, a bit of a whine in his speech.

"I did give you a chance. I let you talk to me. Now go away."

* * * * *

"You're going to burn really bad," Trista said.

"Trista, for the last time, leave it alone."

"Mathyu."

Tosha shook her head and ordered another drink from the cute bartender with the glasses and goatee, wondering if he was a local. Was anyone a local in Florida? When he turned and smiled at her, putting a rum and Coke on the bar, she saw the Chicago Cubs baseball cap on his head. *Nope, yet another guy from the north trying to find some local tail.* She turned back to her sister. "How many times do I have to tell you I'm not going to call you some stupid name you made up in a video game? Sometimes, I hate even calling you sister, you know."

"If you weren't so mean, I would tell you what you just said was mean."

Tosha patted her sister on the back. "And this is why you really get me, sis."

"It's like we're connected in some way. You know, like they say twins are?"

"You're so goofy." Tosha took a sip of her drink. She had to laugh at her sister's often naïve view of the world and her cheesy jokes, but she was the best friend Tosha ever had and would ever

48

have. She couldn't imagine taking this vacation without her. Even when Tosha had a boyfriend (which wasn't too often, if she was being honest with herself, because she usually ran them off when they turned out to be annoying or shallow or just acted like typical guys) she tried to include Trista in the fun.

"Ready for another soda?" the bartender asked.

"Sure. Diet," Trista said.

He squinted, lowering his baseball cap. "Diet? Are you sure?"

Both women laughed.

"How do you think she keeps her girlish figure? I get mine from heavy drinking, Chi-Town boy."

"Chi-Town?" He laughed. "Ahh, I keep forgetting I have my Cubs hat on. It gets so hot back here I switch out this old friend with my Funcoast Bartending one, and a few others I've gotten from vendors over the years. Even though I've been living here over six years, I'll always be a Chicago boy."

"We're from Pennsylvania, on vacation," Trista said with a big smile, lifting her sunglasses and staring at the bartender. "I'm Trista and this is my sister, Tosha."

"Woody. Nice to meet you."

"Like the bartender on *Cheers*, or the cowboy in the *Toy Story* movies?"

"I didn't think anyone remembered *Cheers*, and especially young ladies like yourselves. I wish I was named after the cowboy, too, or at least had Tom Hanks money. Nope, my last name is Woodson."

"What's your first name?" Trista asked.

Tosha had never seen her sis engaging in such casual conversation, especially with a cute guy. She decided to casually fall back and see if her sister had some mojo going.

"Andrew. Ever since I was in school, my friends have always called me Woody. It just stuck, and, by high school, the teachers were calling me it. The only people who call me Andrew are my grandmothers and the cops when I get pulled over."

"That's funny. I think I'll call you Andrew. But not Andy, which is too informal."

"Works for me, Trista." He turned away. "One diet Coke, which you don't really need, coming up."

"What's gotten into you?" Tosha asked when she was sure Woody was out of earshot. "Getting all flirty."

"No, I wasn't. I'm just trying to be nice. I'm a pleasant person. Unlike you, at times."

"Bullshit."

"Always with the profanity."

"Shit, yes. You were practically making out with the guy. I was getting uncomfortable. I didn't know if you wanted me to clear out the place and let you two go at it."

Trista blushed. "That is so not what happened."

"Do I need to get my own room tonight at the hotel, or were you planning on going back to his bachelor pad for the evening?"

"Give me a break. He's nice and I'm nice and we had a two minute conversation about his name. Nothing more."

"But you'd jump his bones in a heartbeat, wouldn't you?"

Trista stared at Woody as he made some drinks. "As you always say, I wouldn't kick him out of bed."

"Haha, I knew it. You still want to leave and go play your stupid game now?"

"I suppose we could hang out another few minutes. You still need to finish your drink."

Tosha picked up her glass. "I can chug it and we can go."

Trista snickered. "I ordered another soda. No use in letting it go to waste."

Woody returned with a diet soda and another rum and Coke for Tosha.

Tosha smiled. "I didn't order this."

"No, but the dude across the bar staring at you was insistent he buy this round, and told me to tell you, if you waved him over to join you and your sister, he'd gladly pick up your bar tab for the day."

Trista glanced across the bar. "Who are they?"

"Stupid Jersey boys. I'm not interested in hanging out with them, even if it will save me a couple of twenties." Tosha turned to Woody. He was cute, and Trista wasn't stupid. "Thanks, but I think I'll pay for this round as well."

"Too late. I added it to his tab." Woody leaned on the counter. "Gladly, too. The one guy isn't a nice guy."

"He seems like a dick," Tosha said.

"That's one way of putting it. Yesterday, I almost had to throw him out of here. He rubs me the wrong way, and I can deal with all kinds of people. I get drunks and nasty people, snobby locals and rich tourists, but this guy is by far the worst. And he's a jerk to his friend."

His friend was cute but Tosha didn't feel like wasting an hour trying to get the idiot out of the picture just to be with some Jersey guy. She could do that back home. "Then I will gladly drink for free and no more."

"Can't say I blame you." Woody moved to his left to take another order.

Trista rubbed the cool sides of her glass. "It's getting really hot."

"Yeah, I agree. I'm getting sweaty, which is not a good look for me. We'll go after this drink."

Trista looked at her sister. "Your shoulders are bright red."

"Whatever. They don't hurt. Ow!" Tosha cried when her sister poked her in the middle of her sunburn. "Don't do that again. Ever."

Trista laughed. "You're like a lobster. You are going to be crying all night."

"Will not."

"Will, too."

Tosha looked over at the two Jersey guys. The cute one was watching the parking lot and the other was staring right at her with a smile. Tosha held up the rum and Coke and mouthed a thank you.

When he pointed at himself and then made a motion to walk around the bar, she shook her head. He suddenly looked pissed. Tosha shrugged her shoulders. He'd taken the chance and he'd failed. Miserably.

"I think it's time to go." Tosha downed the rest of her drink, hoping it would go straight to her head because tonight she was going to be in a world of hurt. A glance at her crimson legs and arms was all she needed to know her sis was right: she'd be up all night crying like a baby.

"Tomorrow you won't make fun of me and you will use sun-block," Trista said.

"Tomorrow will be too late."

Blue Heaven Rendezvous

Woody noticed her from the time she parked her little sports car, put the top up, and strolled confidently to the Tiki bar, knowing all eyes were on her as she moved.

She grinned at several men seated around the bar but didn't say much when they tried to say something witty or carefree to get her attention.

"What'll it be?" Woody asked, knowing how cliché it was to ask, but he felt he had to. He didn't want to stumble over something dumb or try to come up with a funny line off the top of his head and blow it and look stupid in front of those slowly getting drunk around him. He had a reputation to uphold (whether it was true or not) and these guys who frequented the same bar stools, day in and day out, looked up to him, always asking him for advice on dating and how to bag a hot chick. Woody played the part, the happy go lucky guy with the big smile, tossing out jokes and words of wisdom to those who wouldn't remember any of it in the morning.

"I'll have a glass of Chardonnay," she almost whispered. "And I'd like to see a menu."

"But of course." Woody handed her the Golden Lion Café menu. "Will you be joined by someone else? Would you rather get a table?"

She smiled with perfect white teeth. "I'm solo. Why? Can't a girl come to a bar and eat alone? Or do I have to sit down there with the commoners?" She winked at Woody. "I'd much rather sit here and slowly get drunk and enjoy the view."

"That also works. Have you been here before?" Woody asked, casually pointing at the menu and knowing all eyes were on them. There wasn't a sound being made all around the Tiki bar.

"I've been in a few times, but usually sit at the front bar. Today, I decided I wanted something different. What do you suggest?"

Carl, across the bar, snickered. Someone scraped their beer bottle on the counter and someone else shushed them.

"You can't go wrong with the fish and chips. It's our specialty."

She looked at Woody for several heartbeats, and he was successful in not looking away or staring at her cleavage. Eye contact was so important in his job. Obviously, he stared long and hard at a great set when she wasn't looking, and he loved watching the asses go by. But, when they watched him, he watched only the face.

"I'll take it." She handed him back the menu. "It better be good, too," she added.

"Or else?"

She laughed. "Something like that." She glanced at his nametag. "Woody? Really?"

He bowed. "Andrew 'Woody' Woodson at your service."

"Ha. I'm Kerri Woodward. It must be Kismet."

"It must be that or even fate or destiny," Woody said. "Who can say?"

"You're funny, too. I like that."

Woody turned to put in her order and get her wine, and wasn't surprised to see everyone staring at him. He shrugged his shoulders to say 'what?' and it got everyone laughing and talking again.

She was beautiful, a few years older than he was but in such great shape. To the untrained eye, she could pass for late twenties. She obviously worked out, and spent a considerable amount of time and money on her appearance. Woody thought she was doing a fabulous job. Her flowing blonde locks, tipped dark at the ends, perfectly shaped her face. She had smooth skin with just a hint of a suntan. Woody decided she was trying too hard to be noticed. A woman like this had a traveling rich husband and was looking to slum it for a weekend before hubby got home, she was recently divorced and had money to burn on her vices, or she was just not currently attached.

Carl shook his empty beer at Woody with a grin.

Woody placed a glass of wine in front of Kerri and grabbed a cold beer for Carl, ignoring everyone else for the moment. He was sure the comments and questions were going to be rapid fire, and he savored being the center of attention.

"Here you go, Carl."

"Not so fast." Carl leaned forward. "What's your take?"

"On what?" Woody asked, straight-faced. "Your beer? It's good for you. It makes you say stupid things and ask stupid questions."

"I could say the same about you," Carl said. "Don't mess with me." Carl glanced across the bar at the woman. "She doesn't belong here with this group, that's for sure. She slumming?"

Woody glanced back at her. "The thought crossed my mind." He'd been doing this long enough to know she had a good story to tell, and she probably just wanted someone to hear it. Might as well be Woody. "With women like this, you need to be subtle. Let her come to you, and show you her hand. Trust me. I'm on it."

"You'd better share whatever it is," Carl said.

"Share? You think I'd do a threesome with you, Carl?"

It took Carl a second to realize what Woody had said. He laughed and slapped the bar with his hands. "You kill me sometimes."

"Hey, bartender, can I get another drink, today?"

Woody looked over to see the two Jersey boys were still in attendance and the annoying one, named Chazz (really? Was that a real friggin' name? Who named their kid Chazz?), was waving an empty glass. "Today? I suppose." Woody smiled. "How about your friend there, Chazz?"

"How do you know my name?"

"You told it to me either yesterday when you were here, or, maybe, the five times you have mentioned it, today. At some point, it stuck with me. I have a good memory, you know. It helps when it comes to taking orders."

"How about I come across this bar?" Chazz asked, but his friend grabbed him by the arm and told him to calm down. Now.

Woody kept smiling. He wanted these two to go away already. "Can I get you something, Marco? You've been nursing the same beer for an hour."

Marco looked down at his beer. "Yes, I need a shot of something."

Chazz was beaming now. "That's what I'm talking about. Forget the girl and let's get drunk. We only have a few hours before we get on a plane, dude."

Marco closed his eyes and sighed. "I guess so."

Chazz turned to Woody. "Line up four shots of Jack for us, barkeep. Shit, send one over to the hot chick across the bar and this guy here who won't shut up."

Carl laughed and thanked Chazz.

"You got it." Woody grabbed a bottle of Jack Daniels and six shot glasses.

"And one for yourself, too." Chazz slapped his friend on the back. "I knew you'd come to your senses."

Woody put a shot glass on the bar for himself and poured generously. He made sure everyone was good with drinks around the bar, and saw Chrissie come out with the woman's food order. Chrissie smiled at him and gave a quick wave before returning to her tables. Woody couldn't help but watch her go.

"Can I get another Chardonnay?" Kerri asked him.

Woody nodded but hesitated when he made eye contact with the woman, who was doing her best to flirt with her eyes. He wasn't imagining it, either. Her body language spoke volumes. She was hitting on him, and it didn't take stupid lines to do it.

Carl cleared his throat and Woody smiled. It was so obvious and most of the regulars laughed, but then Woody realized Kerri probably thought he was smiling at her. When he put another wine glass in front of her, by the look on her face, he knew she thought he was returning the flirt.

Suddenly, there were glasses to clean and Woody made sure the cooler was properly stocked with cold beers. He saw Chrissie coming by with an empty food tray and waved her over. "I need some beer and more lemons."

"What am I, your slave?" Chrissie asked and stuck out her tongue.

Woody nodded. "Pretty much. Let someone know."

"I'll let Man-Child know."

"That will work." Woody winked at her. "Thank you, ma'am."

Kerri sipped her wine and was staring at Woody. "Is that your girlfriend?"

"Huh? Who?"

Kerri pointed at Chrissie as she disappeared back inside the Golden Lion Café. "I see the way you look at her, and she definitely likes you."

Woody felt his face go red. "How do you know she likes me? I mean... nah, we're just friends. She's cool."

"Wow, you are a horrible liar. It's cool. I get it." Kerri raised her hand and motioned, with her finger, for Woody to come closer.

When he complied, she glanced over at Carl and the others before lowering her voice. "I know you have a reputation to uphold. I get it. I see your monkeys hanging on every word you say. I also see there is something going on between you and the pretty waitress. You just don't know what to do with the information, because she isn't another one night stand for a guy like you. Again, I get it."

Kerri finished her wine in one swallow. Woody went to take her glass and refill it when Kerri put her hand on his.

"I have no problem being just another one night stand. Get it? I'm here for one reason, and it isn't to get drunk on wine. It's up to you. I'm a bored housewife looking to get freaky for one night. I know your reputation as a guy who doesn't kiss and tell. I'm going to leave in a minute and will give you this." She put a business card on the bar and tapped it with a finger. "I got a room at the Flagler Beach Motel. I'm going there now. What time do you get off work?"

Woody checked the clock on the register. "In about forty-five minutes."

"I'll see you then?"

Woody nodded, and smiled when the woman handed him five crisp twenties for her tab and told him to keep the change.

*   *   *   *   *

Marco ordered another beer and was starting to feel good. While Chazz was usually an asshole the drunker he got, Marco was the guy who told everyone around how much he loved them and hugged people. Then he would find a quiet chair and take a nap.

Chazz was looking over the drink menu, asking Woody questions about several drinks and being his normal charming self, making snide comments and pointing out how drinks in New Jersey and New York were different from Florida.

Marco figured the bartender was about done with Chazz, but he was being cool about it, answering his questions and ignoring his stupid comments. Marco put another twenty on the counter and apologized yet again to Woody.

"What's that for?" Chazz asked.

"Because the guy is trying to earn a living, and he has fifteen customers all waiting to order another beer, but you keep bothering him. So I'm paying him so he doesn't toss us out."

"He can try," Chazz said and stared at Woody.

Marco slapped him on the back. "Calm down, killer. We're here to drink and get drunk, remember? Stop trying to fight everyone. It's growing tiresome."

"Why? We've been doing this for how many years? I thought you liked it when I tried to beat everyone up and you had to jump in and save me."

"Never. Not once. And especially while we're on vacation. For once, I want to enjoy a few cocktails and stare at the local women without you being an ass and getting us in trouble."

"I can do it," Chazz said, defensively. He grinned. "I've never actually done it, but I can try, I guess."

"That's the spirit," Woody said, as he put two more beers on the bar. "How long are you boys planning on gracing us with your presence? I heard talk of you flying back to the north and the cold and the snow."

"It's June," Chazz said.

Marco put a hand on his buddy's arm and gave him a look before turning back to Woody. The bartender was going to bust some balls now and Marco didn't really blame him. Chazz had been an ass yesterday and today. "I think he was being funny. To answer your question: we leave tomorrow."

"Nice. Flying out of Jacksonville or Orlando?"

"I don't remember," Marco said and picked up his beer. "It doesn't really matter to me. I just want to get home and forget about Florida."

"What's the matter with Florida, if you don't mind me asking," Carl said, butting into the conversation.

Marco shrugged his shoulders. "I'm... it's just... I need to get home."

"He met a woman," Chazz said.

"Shut up," Marco said, his turn to get defensive. "It's stupid."

Woody grinned and leaned on the counter. "Do tell. We all like a good story."

"I bet it's about a girl you met on the beach and she's from Australia but now it's the end of summer and you need to go back to your school and hang with your greaser buddies and sing," Carl said. "But then she shows up at Rydell High!"

"Idiot," Woody said. "Now tell me the real story."

"You fall in love with a girl but you're a sparkly vampire and she pouts and barely acts," Carl said. "And then a pretty werewolf dude likes you, too!"

"Carl, shut up or you're getting cut off," Woody said.

"Don't threaten me like that," Carl said with a laugh. "Oh, and I need another drink."

Chazz slapped the counter. "The next round for that crazy dude is on me. I'll tell you the real story."

"Shut up, Chazz." Marco didn't want everyone to know his business and wanted to forget about Michelle, as quickly as possible. He looked over at the table she'd been sitting at, with her girlfriend, yesterday and remembered how pretty she was. Even if she was clearly annoyed with his lame excuse for pickup lines. He wanted her out of his head but even now he was thinking about her gorgeous clear eyes and blonde hair and her curves…

"She's this chick he saw here yesterday. She's probably not even a local, just some tourist passing through like him. I didn't see her too well, but he swears she's this super hot chick. She seemed too big for my tastes, but what do I know? I like skinny bitches." Chazz waved at a woman across the bar. "No offense."

"She was here yesterday? When I was here?" Woody asked.

"I was probably here, too," Carl said. "Especially since I was the first customer and closed the place last night."

Woody put his hand on Carl's beer. "That's it, you're cut off."

"I'll be quiet," Carl whined with a smile and Woody let go of his drink.

"She was sitting right there. Big blonde. Her friend was cute. I wouldn't kick her out of bed. Anyway, Marco went over and got shot down in flames. It was brutal."

"You weren't even there. Shut up," Marco said.

"Did you get her number?"

Marco shook his head.

"Did she say anything positive to you?"

Marco shook his head again.

"Shot down in flames," Woody said. "I wonder who she is."

"She said her friends called her Chelle. She made Marco call her Michelle, which is brilliant," Chazz said.

Carl laughed. "Big blonde? Pretty face? Attitude to spare named Michelle? Ha."

"What's so funny?" Marco asked.

"Nothing." Carl looked at Woody. "I'll be quiet."

"For once, you can open your mouth," Woody said.

"Speak," Chazz said. "What do you know, buddy?"

"I know who she is. Michelle Boyd. She drives a red Dodge Charger. Guys hit on her all the time and she never gives them the time of day. Forget her."

"Does she live in town?"

Woody nodded. "She lives off of South Central, down around 18th, I think. Maybe 16th. But I would forget her. She's a tough chick."

"She's worth it," Marco said.

"Oh, I'm not arguing the point. If you like bigger girls, she is a knockout. I love big gals, but she can be tough to talk to. She isn't arrogant but she is very sure of herself." Woody laughed. "Too bad you're leaving tomorrow, too. I would love to see you in action, trying to hit on her again, and her making you cry."

Marco turned to Chazz. "I'm not leaving."

"Please, tell me you're kidding."

"Nope. It's a sign. I'm staying, and you need to keep your mouth shut to Chenzo where I am. Got it?"

"I'm staying then," Chazz said.

"Not a chance. You need to go back, and you know it. Tell them I'm in San Fran or San Diego and I met a girl and I'm retiring and settling down. I'll give them all the codes in an e-mail Monday morning."

Chazz leaned in close to his friend. "This isn't working at a gas station. You can't put in your two-week notice. Chenzo will send someone to kill you."

"And if you really are my friend, they'll think I'm on the wrong coast. Right?"

* * * * *

Woody got into his Chevy Blazer and drove toward A1A. He stopped, waiting for the traffic to thin. He'd had a long day. He gripped the business card from Kerri in his hand and tapped it against the steering wheel.

If he turned right, he'd be heading to the Flagler Beach Motel. To his left and north, he was heading home. Which way to go?

Kerri would be a fun ride, and she didn't look like she wanted more than a one night stand, to feel like a man was interested in her. He was sure her husband was either inattentive or traveling. It didn't really matter. She just wanted to roll around in a hotel room bed and have some fun.

It would be easy to do, and she was really hot. No one would know, and he could simply smile along with Carl and the regulars and not tell them anything.

Woody watched the traffic go by and stared at the beautiful ocean water directly ahead. What should he do?

As he looked back and forth at the traffic, he saw Chrissie, waiting on a table at the front of the Golden Lion Café. She looked over at him, sitting in his car, and smiled with a quick wave.

Woody smiled back and turned left, cutting into traffic and heading home.

Waiting For The Next Explosion

Nichole popped a French fry into her mouth and smiled. "This is the life."

"How's your fish?" her husband Harrison asked. He was about to take another bite of his Philly cheese steak sandwich.

She looked down at her plate of half eaten fish. "I like it. Of course, it's not like back home."

"Is that good or bad?"

"Neither. Just different. Living in New England spoils you for good seafood. That's all I'm saying." Nichole looked out at the beach from their seat on the upper deck in the Golden Lion Café. "It is an amazing view."

"I'm glad I talked you into this."

Nichole laughed. "Um, I think it's the other way around. I talked you into coming to Florida first."

"I'm glad you did." Harrison reached across the table and squeezed her hand. "Three days of sun and fun and then we head to see where I grew up."

Nichole made an exaggerated wrinkling of her nose. "I can't wait to see it."

"I know you don't care, but it is important to me."

Nichole squeezed his hand back. "You do know I'm just teasing you, right? I'm sure New Jersey is really nice. I can't wait to meet everyone. I'm going to need a dress for the funeral."

"There is no funeral. My grandfather has been gone for nearly a month."

"What?"

Harrison glanced at the ocean. It was really beautiful here in Florida. "Yeah, I actually got the word after he'd already been cremated."

"This vacation was on the spur of the moment because you got a phone call your grandfather had *just* died. The way you said it…" Nichole pulled her hands back and put them on her hips. She looked pissed. "You lied to me?"

"No, no way. Why would I lie to you? If my grandfather was really just dead, would we be here in Florida?"

Harrison could tell by the look she was giving him she was processing all the information in her head and, by the way her brow was scrunched up, he knew she wasn't happy with the conclusion she was getting to. "Something doesn't add up," she finally said.

"Alright, I lied to you, but let me explain."

She shot him a dirty look. "Explain? I think you just summed it up."

"By the time I got the word, he was already dead. And cremated."

"Then why are we going to New Jersey? And why fly over a thousand miles in the wrong direction, to Florida first, for three days?"

"We inherited his house."

"And?"

Harrison paused. He knew this could go either way, and he'd known his wife long enough to know she was on the brink of throwing her food at him, creating a scene, and walking off. "I wanted to have a nice vacation, and then go see the house. My family's entire history is in the house, and it is huge. I've seen the pictures. The realtor said we could flip it but we'd be nuts to, because it has so much life to it."

"Holy shit. You've seen pictures?"

"Yes. She was nice enough to e-mail me a bunch of them. I have some on my phone." Harrison pulled out his cell phone when Nichole stood up.

His wife leaned across the table and he could see the fire in her eyes. When she was mad, she yelled. When she was beyond mad, she growled, a guttural sound from her throat. She was growling now. "So, let me get this straight: you thought you'd trick me to go to New Jersey to live there, where you grew up, and without first consulting me about what I wanted to do… but first, you figured a nice vacation to Florida so I'd drop my guard and be all smiles when the realtor handed you the keys? Did you even, for once, consider my feelings on this major move?"

"Yes, of course." Harrison was starting to sweat. "I just thought it would be easier if we went and took a look around. I was going to show you Keyport and where my family came from and let you decide. I just know how you are…"

"What does that mean? How am I, Harrison? Enlighten me. How am I?" She was fully standing now, her hip bumping the table and spilling some of his Coke.

"You know what I mean."

"Give me the hotel room key."

"Honey, sit down. Finish your dinner and then we'll figure it out."

"The key. Now."

Harrison knew people at the adjacent tables were casually watching them now, and he didn't want to fight with her in public. He'd never win, anyway. "I screwed up, but there's a simple solution to this, honey."

"Don't honey me."

Harrison handed her the hotel key card. "Let me pay the bill and then we can leave."

"Oh, I'm already leaving," she said over the shoulder. "You might want to take your time coming back to the hotel, or you might find your pillows in the parking lot."

Harrison could only smile, embarrassed, as the customers around him stared. He couldn't get his wallet out or signal the waitress fast enough.

* * * * *

Knowing his wife was dead serious, he decided to give her some space and stayed at the Golden Lion Café, going downstairs, from the deck, and sitting at the front bar, with his back to A1A and the Atlantic. He would have a few drinks and kill some time before taking the walk of shame to the Flagler Beach Hotel.

The gentleman sitting next to him gave a quick nod of his well-worn hat and went back to staring into his beer. "You can find out a lot about a man by the beer he drinks," the man said.

Harrison decided to answer the man, who was in his sixties with graying stubble and a warm smile. He looked like Denzel Washington, Harrison thought. "I'm drinking a Corona Light."

"Ah, the beer men drink after they've had a fight with their wife or girlfriend. I know it all too well." The man extended his hand. "I'm Dave."

"Nice to meet you, Dave. I'm Harrison."

"From your accent, I'm going to guess you're not from around here," Dave said.

"No. I'm originally from Jersey and living in Massachusetts. We're down here on vacation. Tell me more about my choice of beer," Harrison said. He was fascinated how the man could know anything based on a drink order, but he was right so far.

"The wife is obviously mad and feeling like you tricked her into coming down to Florida under strange circumstances. Am I right so far?"

"Yes," Harrison admitted. He sipped his beer. "Go on."

"I'm going to say it's a death in your family. Your grandfather. He's been cremated and you made it seem like he just died. You brought her to Florida for a few days in order for you to get her buttered up with surf and sand before springing it on her about moving to New Jersey and giving up her life in Mass."

"Holy shit, Dave. Are you a mind reader? What's the trick?"

Dave pointed a finger in the air and smiled.

"God told you?"

"No, you did." Dave looked up. "You were sitting right above me. I was at the table right there finishing my early dinner and heard every word carried on the wind. I might have lost some of my strut over and my eyesight over the years, but the hearing is still intact. Except when my wife is yelling at me for eavesdropping on conversations."

"It's a neat trick. You had me going."

"I could tell by the amazed look on your face." Dave turned to the bartender. "I'll have another Red Stripe, and put his Corona on my tab."

"You don't have to do that," Harrison said. "But I'm not going to fight you over it. In fact, I'll be having another on your tab."

"I think you earned it. You might as well have another beer before you go to the hotel and the firing squad."

"Ah, spoken like a man who knows a thing or two about marriage."

"But of course. We've all been there. Some of us get deeper into the shit, and others... like myself... choose to skirt around the fighting as much as possible. I choose to have another beer," Dave said and raised his new Red Stripe.

Harrison held his Corona up to tap glasses.

Dave smiled. "Eye contact, my friend."

"Huh?"

"When you raise a toast and make new friends, it's always important to make eye contact when you clank your drinks and salute the past and the present."

Harrison laughed but did as he was told. "That's quite the system you have going there, Dave."

"If we don't have traditions, no matter how inconsequential or seemingly small, we fail as a society. We fail as human beings."

"Wow, that's pretty deep."

"I might be getting drunk, so don't mind me."

"I might be joining you, kind stranger with an open bar tab."

"Oh, we shared a round and made eye contact. We're no longer strangers. We've come here to share experiences, and to bond as men. We're also going to get drunk and tell lies and a handful of almost-truths and kill an hour or three."

"What do you do for a living, when you aren't being the local watering hole philosopher?"

"I'm retired. You might even say I'm a bum but I'm not homeless. Does that make sense?"

"Nothing today makes sense. This is a nice place. Come here often?"

Dave laughed. "Son, that sounds like a pickup line. We're friends but not that friendly, if you catch my drift."

"I knew, as soon as I said it, those words were not the right ones."

"I'll let you reset."

"Is this the local hangout you frequent?"

"One of them. Yes. I enjoy being this close to the beach and the waves and the beer."

"There are plenty of nice-looking women, as well," Harrison said.

Dave grinned. "I'm too old to notice the young girls." He tipped his Red Stripe back and drank. "Of course, it may be I'm too old for them to notice me."

"I feel the same way."

"Nah, you're a young man. Wait until your sixties creep up and slap you around. It's not fun rolling out of bed with bones this brittle and old."

"What can we do?" Harrison asked rhetorically.

Dave lifted his Red Stripe. "We can keep drinking, until we have to head over to the motel room and let our wives scream at us for a few hours. Oh, wait… I get to sit here and drink some more. My wife is in love with me today. At least, that's the way I remember it."

"You're truly a lucky man."

Dave raised a finger. "For this one day. Remember that. Tomorrow is Sunday, and it make take on an entirely new context when it comes to male-female relations. Besides, my wife went to visit her son in Atlanta. I'm a free man until noon tomorrow. So, I sit and I drink and I talk with random strangers until they are no longer strangers. It's a fine system, and it keeps me out of trouble."

The two men sat in silence and watched the customers come in and out, finishing off another two beers in the process.

Tommy, the owner of the Golden Lion Café, came out of his office and grabbed a glass of Coke. He smiled at the two men. "Having a good time, mates?" he asked.

Dave raised his Red Stripe. "Nothing could be finer, sir."

"Good. Nice to hear." Tommy drank from his cup. "Well, you fine gents have a nice night."

"You leaving already?" the bartender asked Tommy.

"No. I was going to go home and spend time with the wife, but she went out to dinner with her friends. Instead, I'll dive back into this novel I'm writing. I think I'm almost done with it."

"What's it about?" Harrison asked, knowing he was stalling.

Dave, obviously, knew it as well. He put a hand on Harrison's shoulder. "I think it a fine time to get those walking shoes pointed in the right direction. If you kill anymore time, you're only going to get her mad all over again."

Harrison sighed. "You're right." He finished the last swig of his beer. "Save my seat, just in case she tosses me out."

"She won't. You know why?"

"I haven't got a clue," Harrison admitted.

"Because you are going to admit you were wrong, and you're going to take her out for a nice dinner later tonight at Flagler Fish

Company. Then you're going to take a walk on the beach and kiss your woman under the stars and the moon. And why?"

Harrison smiled. "Because I screwed up. And now I need to make this all about her."

"That's the spirit," Tommy added and slapped the bar. "Good luck."

"I'll have another Red Stripe in your honor, my new friend. I hope not to see you back here. Besides, another stranger will take the spot and I can start all over again," Dave said.

Harrison started the lonely walk back to the hotel room, hoping she wasn't too mad at him. And hoping his pillow wasn't in the parking lot.

A Lot To Drink About

Sophia was having one of those days, when every customer was happy and tipped well, and everything coming from the kitchen or one of the bars was perfect. In the restaurant business, you didn't get days like these too often, and you took advantage of it.

"What are you smiling about?" Chrissie asked her. They stood near the kitchen doors, counting their cash tips.

"I think I already have enough for my trip to Vegas," Sophia said. "I'm excited."

"When are you leaving?"

"Three weeks."

Chrissie counted her tips. "I think I can cover my rent, which is late, of course. Something has to change. I'm doing this all wrong."

"You are, because you're one of the better waitresses," Sophia said.

"Nah."

"Seriously. Most of the waiters and waitresses see the big tips you get. You make more than the rest of us. Honestly, all of the new girls coming in look up to you," Sophia said.

"You're going to make me blush. I'm just trying to keep my head above water. My student loans and car payments are ridiculous. My rent is crazy, and I don't even have cable in my house. I'm still living with my mom. What am I doing wrong?"

Sophia laughed. She genuinely liked Chrissie, because she wore her emotions on her sleeve, in the open, and wasn't good at hiding them. "You can start by calming down. It's a gorgeous night. Live for the moment and put a smile on your face, pretty girl. You have more than money to live for, you know."

"Right now I can't think of anything I have to live for," Chrissie said.

"Really? Not even a cute bartender you've been staring at for months?"

Chrissie's face was red. "No idea what you're talking about. I gotta go back to work." She ran off and left Sophia to pocket her money with a laugh. It was obvious to everyone in the Golden Lion Café; Chrissie and Woody were going to hook up at some point. The only thing stopping her was probably the bartender's horrible reputation as a ladies man and a bit of a dog. Sophia would tell her to live for the moment if she asked her, but she thought Chrissie already knew what was up.

Sophia delivered food to a four top and asked an elderly couple if they needed anything else. The gentleman smiled at his wife and clasped her hand. "Did I hear you say you're going to Las Vegas?"

"Yes, sir," Sophia said. "I've never been. My girlfriend and I have been talking about it for years, and we decided to just throw caution to the wind and take the trip."

"We just came back from Vegas," his wife said and held up her hand, showing off a large wedding ring. "We renewed our vows. We got married in Vegas twenty-five years ago."

Sophia smiled. "Wow! That is very cool."

"The first time we got married we'd known each other for seven hours. We just fell in love at first sight. I knew the first time I saw her I needed to be in her life," he said.

"I was there with friends. I wasn't even supposed to go, but, at the last minute, my daughter physically put me on the plane from Cleveland. I kicked and screamed all the way to Vegas," she said.

"The funny part was I grew up in Cleveland. I lived sixteen miles from where she grew up and went to the rival high school. We graduated within three years of each other."

She patted his hand. "I dated his older brother's best friend briefly. Yet, we'd never met. We drove across the country to meet one another. Doesn't God work in mysterious ways?"

Sophia nodded. "He always keeps us on our toes."

"We met, spent a few hours together and realized it was fate. We were both divorced, both had older children who were starting to go out on their own, and both had good jobs and good pensions. We just did it."

"Elvis married us," she said. "I've always been a big fan of The King."

He laughed. "But this time I got to pick who married us, since you have so many choices in Vegas."

"Who'd you pick?"

"I picked Elvis again, but this time he was a midget," he said. "The wedding picture went on the mantle next to our first one. I can't wait for the grandkids to see it. They always laugh at the original one."

"We retired to Florida two years ago when Bob... oh, how rude... I'm Judith and this is Bob... he turned sixty-three and we decided these old bones had had enough of the cold Ohio weather."

"That sounds so exciting," Sophia said. She wiped a tear from her eye. "Look at me. I'm crying; it's such a great story."

"We think so," Bob said. "We know you're busy, so we'll get out of your hair. Can I get the check?"

"Of course." Sophia dropped their check on the table. "It was nice meeting both of you, and good luck on another twenty-five years. Maybe next time a female Elvis marrying you?"

"I'm thinking Tom Jones," Judith said.

Bob put a pile of cash on the check and handed it to Sophia. "Do me a favor."

"Sure."

"Take some of this tip and put it on black when you get there." Sophia nodded. "I will do that."

"Maybe there's a reason you're going out there," Judith said. "A nice man, perhaps. You might just meet the love of your life."

Sophia thanked the couple and wondered what her girlfriend would say about her meeting a nice man in Vegas.

When she cashed out the bill, she was stunned. The couple had given her a hundred dollar tip.

* * * * *

Brent ordered another Yeungling, on tap, and glanced at the appetizers on the menu. He wasn't sure if he wanted to eat, or just get drunk tonight. His week had been long and he needed to let off some steam without the distraction of his life or his girlfriend right now.

He stood near the front bar and watched the steady stream of cars go by on A1A, a handful of motorcycles thrown in for good measure. Initially, he was going to hang out at Johnny D's but it was his usual spot and tonight he didn't want to engage in long conversations about anything. He'd decided to take the Harley for a spin today and get a solo dinner. Now, holding his second beer, he decided to have a liquid supper and head home.

Brent usually stayed in Palm Coast, preferring some of the local watering holes near his house, like Farley's Irish Pub in European Village, but the lure of the open road was too much for him. "I should have gone to Saint Augustine," he murmured. It would have been a longer ride. He was already getting antsy being in Flagler Beach, and he knew why.

His dad lived in Flagler Beach, and he could usually be spotted in the Golden Lion Café, sitting at the Tiki bar, getting hammered. Johnny D's was a safe bar to hang out in because his dad wasn't a bike rider, and rarely hung out with the biker crowd. He preferred to hang out with other drunks.

Brent sipped his beer as he walked slowly through the crowded dining area, eyes on the Tiki bar. The Golden Lion Cafe got more crowded the later it got; a Saturday night with perfect Florida weather got everyone out.

The Tiki bar was crowded, one side three deep with customers waiting to order a drink. Brent went past the small stage erected in the courtyard, a band, dressed in sixties outfits, was setting up. The lead singer, a skinny blond guy, had a red scarf wrapped around his neck despite the heat. One of the guitarists was dressed in black and had an intense look to him. Brent nodded to the band as he walked past and they returned it.

"What do you guys play?" Brent asked the singer.

"Surf music with a bit of a fun punk edge. I'm Vern," the singer said. "Covers and originals. I hope you stick around; we'll be going on in about five minutes."

The Cherry Drops, according to the logo on their bass drum. Brent decided he'd find a spot somewhere near the stage and order another couple of beers. It might be a better night sitting here than sitting on his couch, watching boring television, and he couldn't remember the last time he was out of the house. His girlfriend was beginning to annoy him and he knew it wouldn't be long before he had enough and broke up with her.

His dad wasn't sitting at the Tiki bar so Brent grabbed a table adjacent with a nice view of the band. A pretty waitress came over and asked if he wanted another beer and he nodded. He slumped down in his chair and got ready to enjoy an uncomplicated night of music and beer, and wished he had more of these in his life.

The band started playing, diving into an original song (he assumed it was since he didn't recognize it) and thought they sounded like REM meets the Beach Boys. Good stuff.

"Brent?"

He turned with a sigh. It was his dad standing behind him.

"Can I sit?" his dad asked.

"No." Brent turned back to the band. As soon as he saw the waitress again, he'd pay for his beer and go home. The fun was over.

He wasn't surprised when his dad pulled a chair close to him and sat down. "How have you been?"

"What do you care?" Brent asked, crossing his arms and looking around for the waitress. He saw her and got her attention.

"I'm your dad. Of course, I care."

"You always had a funny way of showing me you cared. In twenty-two years, I barely heard a sound from you even though we live a town away from each other."

"I know I haven't been the best dad."

"No shit. You might be winning the votes for worst dad, though. At least you have that," Brent said. "I told you last time to forget I exist. I've done it about you and it's working out nicely so far."

"I know I've made mistakes."

Brent threw up his hands. "Man, I've heard these lame excuses and clichés so many times I can probably save you the breath and run them through my head. It doesn't change a thing. You walked out on me and mom when I was two. Twenty years later and I can count the number of times I've seen you, and, when I do, you want me to buy you a beer and pretend everything is water under the bridge. Guess what? I'm not interested in being your drinking buddy. I'm not interested in the same tired excuses, and I'm not going to sit here and share a couple of beers and watch the band with you."

The waitress came over but when she heard the venom from Brent she hesitated.

"We'll get another round, Sophia. Put it on my tab."

The waitress smirked. "Carl, you don't have a tab. Remember?"

He pulled out a twenty and handed it to her.

"I don't want another beer." Brent stood. "I'm not doing this with you, so forget it. This isn't how this turns out. You don't get to buy me a lousy three dollar bottle and we sit around and cry to each other about how fucked up our lives became, and why it got to this. You don't get to come back into my life, because I'm better off without you. Carl."

Brent knew calling him by his first name was a slap in the face, and he was glad. He was angry, and he knew he was making a scene. Despite the band drowning most of it out, people were staring.

The last time they'd run into each other was in Publix in Palm Coast and Brent had called him Carl. His dad acted like he'd been punched in the stomach and Brent didn't care. The bastard deserved it. "I want nothing to do with you. Why is that so hard to understand? I've lived a decent life without a dad. I'm twenty-two. I don't need a father figure in my life now. Mom did a hell of a job without you. I can't imagine how shitty my life would have been with a drunken dad in it."

"I would love to make amends," Carl said.

The waitress was still standing there, unsure how to proceed. Carl told her to bring two more beers.

"Fine, I get it. I'm a shitty dad and a shitty person. Can you at least sit down? Let me buy you a beer." Carl looked around at the people staring. "You're embarrassing yourself."

Brent sat down and was instantly mad he had. Why was he wasting his time? He turned to watch the band as they started another song he didn't recognize but sounded great. He'd need to check these guys out in the future. Maybe they had a CD for sale. Before he left, he'd need to find out.

"I'll sit here and have a beer and watch the band as long as we don't have to talk. Deal?" Brent asked, not even looking at his dad.

"I can live with that. It's a step in the right direction."

"No, there is no direction. We aren't friends and we aren't family. You lost both those privileges twenty years ago when you screwed over my mother and became the town drunk. You know how many times I've seen your car around town? How many places I refused to go to because I knew you were there?"

"Why'd you come here? You obviously know this is my spot."

"I said we weren't going to talk, but I have to vent and you have to listen, or I walk right now," Brent said.

"Then walk."

"Huh?"

Carl smiled as the waitress put two beers down on the table and walked away quickly. "You think you're going to sit here all night and get on your high horse and bitch about what a shitty dad I was, and I'm supposed to take it? Screw that. I've tried to talk to you but you don't want to hear it. I can't say I blame you, but if you think I'm not going to defend myself from your attacks, you're really not my son. Right or wrong, I don't have to sit here and take this shit." Carl pointed to the exit. "Regardless of whether you talk to me or not, whether you sit here and shut the hell up and drink a beer and listen to the band, I'm going to enjoy my beer. And the next one, and the one after. Because I'm an alcoholic and I've given up everything I love in my life for this beer in my hand. And I'm not going to change. I'm going to die drunk and I've made peace with God about it. But you need to get over this anger or it will eat you up inside and kill you, same as I'm dying from the alcohol poisoning my body."

"Then I'll ignore you and you ignore me and I'll listen to The Cherry Drops." Brent picked up the beer from the table and took a long pull from it, turning to watch the band. Now it was a matter of pride. He wasn't going to let this man get under his skin anymore.

The other guitarist in the band was rocking out, his Elvis Costello glasses almost coming off his head as he jammed. The bass player looked like George Harrison's son and the drummer like an extra from *Animal House*, a big older guy who was pounding the drums. They were playing a song now with a chanting chorus and it took Brent a second to realize it was from the television show *Laverne & Shirley*.

He turned to his dad, who was singing along with the band and shaking his beer.

Brent stood and walked away. He wasn't mad anymore, but he didn't want to share a happy moment with Carl, the bastard who'd taken so much from him when he walked out. And the man who was in love with the beer in his hand and not his family.

Come To The Moon

The sun was gone, fallen away from the ocean to the west. With the darkness came a cool breeze off the Atlantic, the Tiki torches flickering and lanterns swaying as they cast light onto the Golden Lion Café. It was another perfect night to get dinner and a drink and mix in with the locals and tourists.

Mac and Ginny sat and sipped their drinks on the upper deck, admiring the waves across the street. Sophia delivered their order of chips and salsa.

"You really want to do this?" Mac asked his wife. "You sure?"

Ginny reached across the table and gripped her husband's hand. "Yes, honey. We spent last night talking about this. The new house is gorgeous, and you heard what Beverly said."

"Yeah, I know. We can get the house in Flagler Beach for a song and dance. I get it. I'm not worried about that part. And I'm sure she can sell our house in Palm Coast in a heartbeat. I'm just worried."

"About what?"

Mac smiled. "About the old house, and the memories we have there. Marie and Brandon were both born there, and we spent so many Christmases and Thanksgivings in that dining room."

"And me in the tiny kitchen," Ginny said.

Mac grinned. "You know what I'm getting at. What do you think Marie is going to say when she finds out?"

"Finds out what?" their daughter said as she walked up and sat down next to Ginny. "What did you two do now?"

Mac looked at Ginny. "See? I didn't want to do it this way."

"Do what?" Marie asked. She helped herself to their chips and salsa and waved over Sophia. "Can I get a sweet tea and fish and chips, please?"

"Who's paying for that?" Mac asked.

"You. And you are my loving parents, who obviously did something pretty bad. So, spill your guts, old man."

"There is a time and a place for family discussions, and sitting here is not the time or the place. We'll sit down tonight when we get home," Mac said and adjusted his baseball cap before polishing off his beer.

"Are you two getting a divorce?" Marie asked sarcastically. "Mom, can I stay with you? Dad snores too much."

"So does your mother."

"What?" Ginny asked.

"Nothing, dear." Mac closed his eyes and sighed. "Your mother and I are very happy together."

"Very? I think you're stretching it now," Ginny said and laughed.

Mac threw up his hands. "Fine, whatever… we kinda like each other, and it would be too much work to have your mom move out. Besides, she'd miss me too much. I am quite a catch."

"And, when we move, we'll be doing it together," Ginny added.

Mac slapped the table. "Ginny, I just told you I called a family meeting for when we got home."

"And since Mom is the real wearer of the pants, she decided to tell me now." Marie looked up as Sophia put her food on the table. "Thank you." She turned back to her dad. "And you can talk while I stuff my face. Win/win."

"We are thinking of selling the house," Mac said.

Marie's eyes went wide. "And move where? Not back to Tennessee or California?"

"Flagler Beach. A few blocks from Kokomo's Café, going south," Ginny said.

"Awesome," Marie said and popped a French fry into her mouth. "Living on the beach will be cool."

Mac shook his head. "I'm sitting here worried you're going to freak out about it."

"Why should I? I'm a young, single girl living on the beach now. There isn't anything better than that. I can walk out my front door and hit the beach. No more driving and loading up the car, no more worries about time and stuff."

Mac grabbed one of her fries and stuffed it in his mouth.

"I told you she wouldn't freak. She is so my daughter. Brandon will have a fit, since he is definitely like his dad," Ginny said.

"I can't argue with that. He doesn't even live with us anymore, yet he'll still go crazy. And we'll be around the corner from the café, and him, at Flagler Fish Company. Even closer and another excuse for Brandon to pop in and get some food." Mac ordered another round of drinks when Sophia came over.

"Are we really moving?" Marie asked.

"There's a lot of work to be done, so I don't want anyone to get their hopes up. We looked at the house last night and your mom really likes it, and so do I. Obviously, the view of the ocean is amazing, and, if I was in the mood, I could walk or ride my bike to work. Not that I ever will, but there is the option. But Beverly only walked us through it and told us the price. She still has to put in a formal bid for us. Then there is the fun of selling our house. We have someone interested who already has the necessary money to buy it, so, initially, it looks favorable. But there is so much paperwork to be done, and, at any point, someone could back out or money could fall through the cracks or a hundred other things could happen."

"What your dad is trying to say is: yes, we'll be moving as soon as we can."

* * * * *

Chrissie was exhausted. Her shift had been long but without incident, and she genuinely loved her job. But she needed to get off her feet and relax.

"Anything fun going on tonight?" Man-Child asked her, not looking in her direction.

Chrissie smiled. She knew the kid had a crush on her and he was really nice, but way too young. In time, he'd grow to be a heartbreaker. He just needed to gain some confidence and date girls his own age, even though he looked much older with his big size and a full goatee. She'd seen teenage boys like him working at restaurants like this, and, as they got older and had a couple of lucky rolls in the hay with a loose waitress or two, they grew into themselves. She hoped Austin didn't do it too quickly, because his charm was in the fact he wasn't an arrogant jerk. He was just a cute kid who would someday be a man.

"My night will consist of pajamas, a bowl of popcorn and a rom-com starring Jennifer Aniston," Chrissie said. She checked the clock on the wall. "I have two minutes before I can get out of here, and I can't wait."

"I like her movies."

"What's your favorite?" Chrissie asked to make conversation but realized, from the look on Austin's face, she'd caught him just trying to agree with her. "I mean, they're all good to me."

"Um, yeah," he finally said. "Okay, I gotta go clean off ten." He started to walk away but stopped. "You have a good night. I'll see you later."

"You have a great night, too, Austin."

"Thank you," he said.

"For what?"

"For always being cool with me. And for not calling me Man-Child to my face. It bothers me when some of the guys say it. I don't know who came up with the nickname, but I hate it."

Chrissie grinned. "Someday you'll be older and no one will remember calling you some stupid nickname. It won't fit anymore."

"I wish."

"Trust me. I was called some pretty bad names in school."

"I doubt it," Austin said and looked like he wanted to run away.

"I was. But I got over it and some of the names went away. The rest I'm glad people forgot about. And it's what will happen to you, too."

"Thanks," Austin said. Chrissie turned away to pretend she was looking at the phone list for employees so he could, gracefully, walk away.

When he did, she smiled. He was a good kid.

Chrissie realized she was staring at the list, her eyes dropping to the bottom. *Andrew Woodson.* She stared at his cell phone number. She knew it by heart, although she'd never called it. How many times had she been here, after a shift, and memorized his number?

"Honey, are you staring at the phone list again?" Sophia asked as she walked up.

"No... huh?"

Sophia laughed. "Wow, you are really bad at this. Can I ask you a serious question?"

"Can I say no?"

"Not even an option. Why is it taking so long for you and him to just do something about this?"

"I don't understand."

"The hell you don't. A blind man can see you two like each other."

"I don't think he likes me." Chrissie looked away. "And he's such a man-whore."

"You know this from personal experience?"

"No. I just see the way he is around women."

"Flirty and always smiling and pouring them drinks and getting great tips. Like we do around dudes who we know shell out money, right? It's all a game, and Woody is one of the best. Everyone talks about him. The women throw themselves at him and the guys want to be him." Sophia put an arm around Chrissie's shoulders. "But look around. How many of these waitresses like him? Quite a few. How many of them have told you they slept with him or gave him head behind a dumpster?"

"Eww, Sophia, you are always so gross."

"How many?"

Chrissie thought about it. "None."

"Exactly. I've been watching him and he is a class A flirt, and his tips are amazing. Probably the best in Flagler County and definitely in Flagler Beach. Yet... when the regulars try to get the juicy gossip on certain women, or think he's nailed another one of us, he smiles and ignores them and let's their imaginations run wild."

"Then I should talk to him?"

Sophia reached in Chrissie's pocket and pulled out her cell phone. "Call him. Now."

"No way. I'll wait until I see him and then I'll talk to him. I swear."

"You're only lying to yourself. I don't care. I'm just trying to help, but I don't need to play matchmaker. It's already happened but one of you needs to take the first step."

"I can't."

"Yes, you can. I'm sure you have the number already programmed in this phone." Sophia started hitting buttons and Chrissie snatched it from her. "Am I right?"

Chrissie smiled. "Of course. But I would never call." She groaned. "What if he doesn't answer? What if he's out on a date? What if he has a live-in girlfriend?"

"What if he's a serial killer? What if he's hanging with his murderous bike gang? What if he's got some weird fetish for armpits?"

"There is something wrong with you."

"I've been told by better people than you," Sophia said. "Look, I'm going to go back to work. You have the rest of Saturday night ahead of you. Spend it alone or spend it with the guy you've been crushing on for months. Up to you."

Sophia walked away.

Chrissie remembered when he'd left before and how he'd waved and smiled at her. Maybe he wasn't a bad guy, and maybe his bad reputation was something he didn't bother changing because it helped him keep his distance.

She decided to call him.

Woody picked up on the first ring.

*　*　*　*　*

Tommy looked up, at the clock in his office, through swollen eyes. It was two minutes to midnight. He smiled. "I bloody did it," he muttered, his mouth dry. He eyed the unopened bottle of rum on his desk but decided he needed something a bit lighter: water or a Coke.

He knew when he snuck home and tried to crawl into bed with his wife there'd be hell to pay, but right now he didn't care. He was elated. Tommy went into the main restaurant bar and turned on a couple of lights so he didn't trip on something and get hurt. He laughed at the rich irony. Someone finding him dead on his own bar floor, completely sober, would be amusing. Maybe not for Tommy but for the openers.

The bar was closed up so, after he poured himself a soda, he took the walk up the stairs to the top deck and sat down at a table overlooking A1A.

Tommy wished he'd grabbed a bag of chips and some salsa but he was too relaxed to get back up and go down for them. Instead, he lit two candles and sipped his Coke and smiled, watching the moonlight on the waves and listening to the beautiful rhythmic sound they made as they crashed on the sand.

He was finished and he was content.

A flashlight beam caught him in the face from below on the sidewalk. "Who's up there?"

Tommy shielded his eyes. "Turn off the blasted light, it's Tommy."

The light remained pointing at him. "Tommy who?"

"Tommy, the bloody owner of the Golden Lion Café. Who are you?"

The light moved away from him but was still on. "Sorry. I thought it was you."

"Then why'd you keep the bloody light on me face? How many men, in Flagler Beach, do you know with such a different accent?"

"At least three. Sorry."

"Ah, no worries." Tommy looked closer, as he leaned over the rail. "Is that Travis Armstrong I see?"

"Yes, sir. I'm sorry. Just doing my job."

"Don't be silly. I'm glad you coppers are watching my place, I really am. Come on up and have a drink with me."

"I can't. I'm on duty."

"Nonsense. I'm drinking Coke. I'll get some chips and salsa and we can get some soda. I'll be right down."

Tommy skipped down the steps two at a time and unlocked the front partition. "Come in, come in."

Travis smiled. "I can't stay long. I'm supposed to be watching for speeders."

Tommy looked north and south down A1A. "I suppose you need actual cars driving on the road for that to work, eh? Sit down… no, better yet, go upstairs. I have wonderful news and it's late and I need someone to share it with."

Once he'd gotten the food and drink, Tommy joined Travis.

"How have you been? Catching the bad guys?" Tommy asked.

Travis grinned. "We had some fun with a bike gang yesterday, but it wasn't anything. It never is."

"I heard they found a body under the pier?"

"We found some bones, but I wasn't on duty then. I'm not sure what happened. I'm sure, by the time I find out, the entire town will know."

"Good news and gossip travel fast." Tommy held up his cup of soda. "Here's to a good life."

"Amen to that." Travis drank half of the soda in one pull before setting it back down on the wooden table. "So, what's the good news you want to share?"

"Oh, right!" Tommy rubbed his hands together. "I finished my bloody book."

"You wrote a horror novel? Like that zombie guy everyone is talking about?"

"No, no," Tommy said and laughed. "I wrote an epic tale of romance, freedom and beaches. It's like a Jimmy Buffett song, come to life, on the written page."

"It sounds interesting."

"It is, and not just because I wrote it. I'm done now. Finally. Now I can rest and stop beating myself up over it. I'll need a proper edit, of course. But the hard part is over."

"Not really," Travis said.

'What do you mean? I finished the book, lad."

"And that is awesome. Congratulations. Except…"

"What? Spit it out."

"My buddy's uncle is an author in Palm Coast, and he says the easy part is writing the book. The hard part is getting sales on it, publishing it yourself or with a publisher… and the constant marketing you have to do. Plus, the best you can do is jump right back into writing and get the next book written."

"Aww, let me enjoy my night," Tommy said with a laugh. "I've just written the greatest book anyone's ever written. Let me have my moment in the sun." He pointed up. "My moment in the moonlight, as it stands." Tommy smiled and raised his half-empty soda cup. "This deserves another toast."

Author Notes

After the success of the *Kokomo's Café* stories, I wanted to keep the momentum going. That first set of stories is set on one day (a Friday) and I decided the second book would be all set on the following day, a Saturday.

The first story naturally begins with the opening rituals of the Golden Lion Café, and introduces the reader to a few characters that will be in and out of the 10 stories, including owner Tommy.

The second story centers around Bethany and Colleen, two characters I've written about before, in my zombie novella set just up the road: *Dying Days: The Siege of European Village* (co-authored with fellow local writer Tim Baker).

You'll also find some recurring characters from the *Kokomo's Café* stories as well as new friends unique to this set of tales, and ones you'll be following along on their continued journey through Flager Beach Florida.

The third story here is actually based on a true story Golden Lion Café owner Tony told me when we first talked about me doing this book, where a guy sitting at the bar was suddenly chased by the police and dove into the ocean. I thought it was funny, and added my own twist as well as some colorful characters that actually frequent the area. The story includes another appearance by Rene, and Captain Rob is here, a version of him as seen in author Tim Baker's latest book *Unfinished Business*. Buy it because it is a great book, and because then he'll buy me banana bread beer with the money.

The fourth story came about because I absolutely love author Bryan Hall's *Southern Hauntings Saga*, and his anti-hero Crate. These stories are must-reads. Dark and descriptive, his ghost stories aren't your normal run of the mill tales. I'm indebted to him for letting me put Crate into my world and tell a unique story.

The fifth story in this release has the fictional versions of two very cool people I know, one who runs (with her amazing husband) J And J Fitness, and the first roller derby chick I ever met who loved the sport and loved to talk about and promote it as much as I like to talk about my books. I put them together to see what would happen, and I'm quite happy with the results. I'm sure you'll see both of them sooner than you think. Like, in the third book, which will be centered on J And J Fitness.

The sixth story features another character from my *Dying Days* zombie series, this time Tosha Shorb, based loosely on a real woman who is just as feisty and is one of the greatest redheads I ever met. We became online friends and she pushed me to give her character the various edges you'll see in her appearance in *Dying Days 2*. Whenever I was worried I was going too far with her fictional likeness she laughed and told me it wasn't enough.

About the seventh story... I'm starting to really dig the Woody character, and will definitely add him to future stories in other great Flagler Beach spots. This story shows a slightly different side to him, and opens him up for many questions about Chrissie and who he really is and wants to be... plus, he's in the middle of the action. Marco and Chazz are also fun characters (along with the absent but mentioned Chelle) and I see a full-blown book about them in the works, so I hope you are looking for it...

The eighth tale features Harrison and Nichole, who started off the *Keyport Cthulhu* series in "Ancient"... this is a loose back-story for when they came to Florida before New Jersey, and it might not synch up 100%, which is the fun of fiction, right? I purposely didn't read "Ancient" again before writing this story. But I hope you read "Ancient"...

With these last two stories, I wanted to wrap up a few ideas and keep some storylines open for future stories set in Flagler Beach. I also pulled in Mac and Ginny from the first book to update readers on their story, and to let you see the progression of certain characters as the days go by.

Some characters will never be seen again, while others will appear in other businesses and days as we move along. Someone said to me the stories were too open-ended and left you wanting more... I say... exactly.

Armand Rosamilia

July 29th 2013

Armand Rosamilia is a New Jersey boy currently living in sunny Florida, where he spends his hard days soaking up the sun, writing about the people he sees and the monsters in his head, and trying to get writing done when there are so many beautiful distractions in his life…

http://armandrosamilia.com for more information!

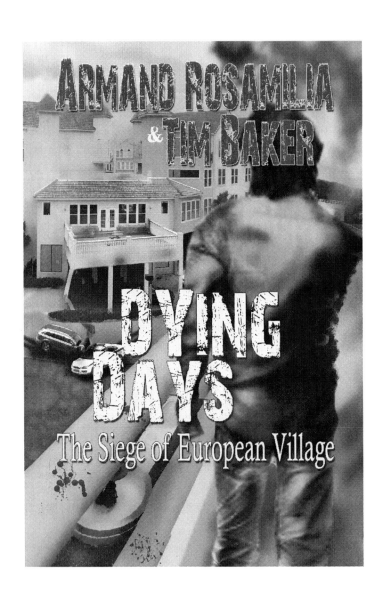

ARMAND ROSAMILIA & TIM BAKER

DYING DAYS

The Siege of European Village

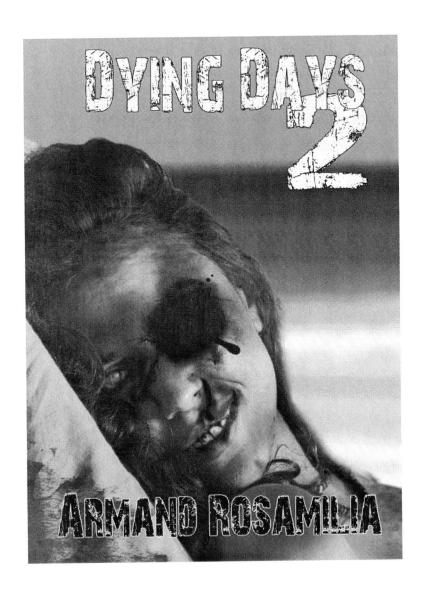

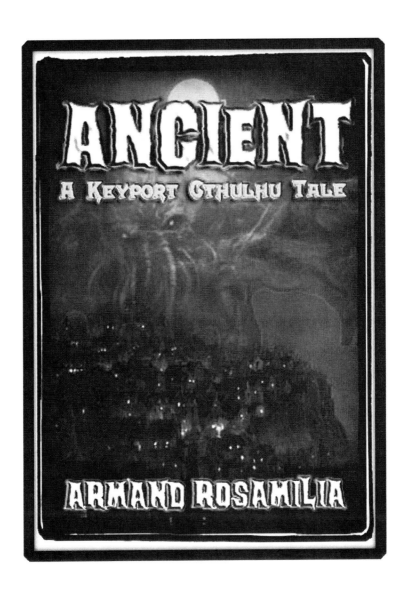

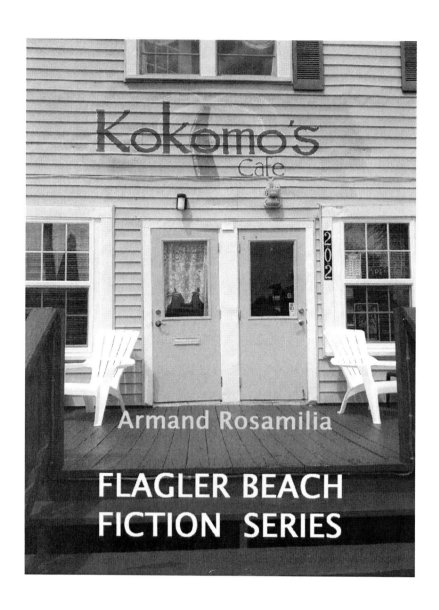

Armand Rosamilia

FLAGLER BEACH
FICTION SERIES